RESCUE RUN

RESCUE RUN

Anne McCaffrey

Illustrated by

Pat Morrissey

79234

The Wildside Press
Newark, NJ

RESCUE RUN

Published by the Wildside Press

The Wildside Press
37 Fillmore Street
Newark, NJ 07105.

ISBN 1-880448-26-0

RESCUE RUN

"MA'AM?" ROSS VACLAV BENDEN said in a surprised tone, "there's an orange flag on the Rukbat system." He swiveled from his position toward the *Amherst*'s command chair and the battle cruiser's captain, Anise Fargoe.

The *Amherst* had been assigned to conduct a determined search through the Sagittarian sector of space for any evidence of new incursions by the Nasties. The punitive war of six decades ago proved insufficient to dissuade those intruders from annexing remote elements of the Federation. There had already been incidents in the Rigel sector despite a powerful Federated force. A massive seek-and-destroy operation was now five years in progress with, mercifully, only a few infiltrations discovered. And those, outposts and two space stations, had been obliterated. Not until all adjoining space and every peripheral system had been investigated and warning devices strategically strewn would the Federation enjoy any sense of security. A second prolonged Nasties Cam-

7

paign would ruin the already depleted Federation. Quick sharp thrusts now, the Combined Joint Staffs had wisely decided, should suffice.

As the *Amherst* had so far had a very boring swing through their sector, Lieutenant Benden's unexpected comment roused everyone on the bridge.

"Orange? This far out?" Captain Fargoe asked, her eyes widening in a flare of excitement. "Didn't know we had colonies in this sector."

'Orange' signified that an investigation should be initiated by any vessel close enough to the flagged system to do so.

"I'm accessing files, ma'am," and Benden, suddenly remembering family history, breathlessly awaited the entry. He tapped his thumbs restlessly on the edge of the keyboard and got a quick repressive glance from old Rezmar Dooley Zane, the duty navigator. "Oh," he added, deflated as the file header informed him that a distress message had been received from the colony on Pern, Rukbat's only inhabitable planet.

8

"Well, let's see the message," Captain Fargoe said. Anything to relieve the tedium of the fruitless search through this deserted — almost deserted — sphere of space. "Screen it."

Benden transferred the message to the main screen.

Mayday! Pern colony in desperate condition following repeated attacks of an uncontacted enemy invasion force employing unknown organism . . .

"Nasties don't *need* germ warfare," muttered brash Ensign Cahill Bralin Nev. Someone else snickered.

. . . which consumes all organic matter. Must have technical and naval support or colony faces total annihilation. There is wealth here. Save our souls. Theodore Tubberman. Colony Botanist.

There was an almost embarrassed silence for the tone of the message.

"Hardly the Nasties then," the cap-

9

tain said dryly. "Probably some old weapon-system has been triggered. Perhaps one of the Sifty units we ran into in the Red Sector. I thought only survivor types were chosen to be colonists. Mister Benden, what does Library say about this Pern expedition?"

Ross didn't need to search for the official documentation on the expedition. He knew most of the tale by heart, but he keyed up the file.

"Captain, a low-tech, agrarian colony was chartered for the third planet of the Rukbat system, under the joint leadership of Admiral Paul Benden —"

"Your uncle, I believe."

"Yes, Captain," Ross replied, keeping his tone level. Proud though his entire family was of Paul Benden's most honorable service record, he had taken a lot of gibing during his first cadet year when his uncle's victory at Cygnus was telecast as a documentary and in his third year when Admiral Benden's strategy was discussed in Tactics.

"A most able strategist and a fine

commander." Fargoe's voice registered approval but her sideways glance warned Benden not to presume on his uncle's sterling record. "Continue, mister."

"— under the joint leadership of Admiral Paul Benden and Governor Emily Boll of Altair. Six thousand-plus colonists, chartered and contracted, were transported in three ships, *Yokohama*, *Buenos Aires*, and *Bahrain*. The only other communication was the regulation report of a successful landing. No further contact was expected."

"Humph. Idealists, were they? Isolating themselves and then screaming for help at the slightest sign of trouble."

Ross Benden gritted his teeth, searching for some polite way to assert that Admiral Benden would not have 'screamed for help' and he bloody well hadn't sent that craven message.

Fortunately, after a moment's thought, the captain went on, "Not Admiral Benden's style to send a distress message of any kind. So, who's this Theodore Tubberman, Botanist, who affixed his name to the plea? A mayday should have been authorized by the colony leaders."

"It wasn't a *standard* capsule," Benden replied, having noted that emendation. "But expertly contrapted. It was also sent to Federation headquarters."

"Federation headquarters?" Fargoe sat forward, frowning. "Why HQ? Why not the Colonial Authority? Or the Fleet? No, if it wasn't signed by Admiral Benden, the Fleet would have shifted it to the CA." Then she sat, chin on one hand, studying the report, scrolling it forward from her armrest key pad. "A non-standard homing device sent to Federation HQ indicating that the colony was under attack . . . hmm. And nine years after a successful landing, forty-nine years ago.

"How far are we from the Rukbat system, Mister Benden?"

"Point 045 from the heliopause, ma'am. Science Officer Ni Morgana wanted a closer look at that Oort cloud. She's interested in cometary reservoirs.

That's when I noticed the orange flag on the system."

"They wanted squadrons then?" The captain gave a short bark of laughter. "Nearly fifty years ago? Hmm. No Nastie activity was noticed that soon after the War. This Tubberman fellow doesn't specify. Maybe that's what he intended. Big unknown alien life form attack might have stirred Federation." She gave a dubious sniff.

"What sort of resources does this Pern have, Mister Benden?"

Benden had anticipated that request and inserted a smaller window on the main screen with the initial survey report. "Pern evidently only had minimal resources, enough to supply the needs of a low-tech colony."

"No, that sort of ore and mineral potential wouldn't have interested any of the Syndicates," the captain mused. "Too costly to use an orbiting refinery or to transport the ores to the nearest facility. Nine years after touchdown? Long enough for those agrarian types to settle

14

in and accumulate reserves. And the EEC doesn't list any predators." She paused in her review of the data and made a slight grimace. "Have Lieutenant Ni Morgana report to the bridge," she said over her shoulder to the communications officer.

The captain tapped her fingers on her armrest, which caused the crew to exchange glances. The captain was thinking again!

"Doesn't compute that Paul Benden would send any distress message," she went on. "So where was he when this Tubberman sent off his contraption? Had the menace from outer space done in everyone in authority?"

"Internal conflict?" Benden suggested, not able to believe his resourceful uncle would have been destroyed by a mere organism after surviving all the Nastie Fleet had thrown at him. That would be ironic. And the Admiral had certainly researched the colonial scheme from every aspect, but he might have relied on Rukbat's isolated position in

Federated space to diminish any hostile attacks. The EEC report listed no hostile organism on the planet. Of course, no one could rule out such a bizarre possibility as an attack by a remnant weapons system. Sections of the galaxy were strewn with the unexploded minefields from ancient wars. Not necessarily of Nastie origin.

The grav shaft whooshed open and Lieutenant Ni Morgana entered, stood to attention and snapped off a salute. "Captain?" and she tilted her head awaiting her orders.

"Ah, Lieutenant, there is not only an Oort cloud surrounding the Rukbat system but it appears to be orange-tagged, distress message," the captain said, gesturing for Ni Morgana to read the data which now occupied several windows on the big screen.

"Coming on a bit thick, weren't they? Alien invasion!" Ni Morgana gave a snort of disgust after a quick perusal. "Although," and she paused, pursing her mouth, "it's just possible that the

16

'unknown organism' has been seeded into the cometary cloud to camouflage it.''

"What are the chances of it containing some engineered organism that attacked the planet fifty years ago?'' Captain Fargoe was clearly skeptical.

"I am hoping that we can obtain samples of the cloud as we pass it, ma'am,'' Ni Morgana replied. "It is unusually close in to the system for an Oort cloud.''

"Have Oort clouds ever been found to harbor natural viruses or organisms that could threaten a planet?''

"I know of several cases where it's always been assumed that inimical mechanisms have been launched from one solar system to another — 'berserkers' they were called.''

"Could the organism this Tubberman mentions be a Nastie softening agent? Destroying all organic matter seems like a weapon of some kind, doesn't it?''

"We've learned not to underestimate the Nasties, Captain. Though their methods, so far, have been much more direct.'' Ni Morgana's smile was tight, understandable when you knew that the science officer was the only survivor of her family, solely because she was at the Academy when the enemy had attacked her home world. "However, since the Nasties have been trying to establish bases far from well traveled space, it becomes a possibility out here."

"Yes, it does, doesn't it," the captain said thoughtfully and then grimaced. It was the ambition of every member of Fleet and EEC from the lowliest long distance single scout to the commander of the heaviest battle cruiser to discover the Nasties' home world, and Captain Fargoe was scarcely an exception.

"Whatever the attack on Pern was, they would not have sent for help unless their situation was desperate," Ni Morgana added. "You are aware that the Colonial Authority exacts punitive payments for such assistance?"

A complex series of expressions rippled across the captain's face. "Far too high for the service they give, and the time it takes them to respond. The colo-

18

nists would be mortgaged body, blood, and breath unto the fourth generation to repay such a debt. Also the message was not sent by Admiral Paul Benden. That's one man I'd like to pipe aboard the *Amherst*."

"He'd scarcely be alive now," Benden heard himself saying. "He was in his seventh decade when he started."

"A good colonial life can add decades to a man's span, Benden," the captain said. "So, I think we can entertain a rescue run to Pern. Lieutenant Zane, plot a course that will take us through the system close enough to this Pern to launch the shuttle. We can give the other planets and satellites a good probe on the swing past. Mister Benden, you'll command the landing party: a junior officer and, say, four marines. I'll want your crew recommendations, and calculations on a projected journey to rendezvous with the *Amherst* on her turn back through the system. Allowing, say . . . how long did the EEC survey team take . . . ah, yes, five days and a bit . . .

19

allowing five days on the surface to make contact with the colonists and establish their current situation."

"Aye, aye, Captain," Benden replied, trying hard to keep elation out of his voice. Lieutenant Zane on the navigation board shot him a malevolent glance, which he ignored, as he did Ensign Nev to his right who was all but tugging his sleeve to remind Ross that he'd had xeno training.

"I suggest you talk with Lieutenant Ni Morgana, Mister Benden, when she has completed her survey of the Oort cloud matter. There might just be some connection and these ancient weapons can produce some awkward surprises." She awarded Ross Benden a quick nod. "You have the con, Lieutenant Zane." With that, the captain slid from the command seat and left the bridge.

As Saraidh Ni Morgana took her seat at the science terminal, she winked at Ross Benden, which he interpreted as her support in his assignment.

▼ ▲ ▼

ON THE 3-D GLOBE ON THE *AM-herst*'s bridge, the ship seemed only centimeters from the edge of the nebulosity that was the Oort cloud. As she approached at an angle to sample a core through the thickest part of the cloud, a great net was fired from a forward missile tube on the port side. The net would both collect debris and clear the ship's path. No ship would barrel through such a cloud, where particles were as close as tens of meters. The biggest particles were about a kilometer apart. The problem was to avoid collision of the net with anything above a ton, which would tear it and bring the ship's meteorite defense into play.

During the next two weeks, while the *Amherst* passed beyond the cloud, heading into the Rukbat system, the science officer carefully examined the material. First she asked permission to rig an empty cargo pod with remote waldo controls and monitors. A work party towed the pod out to a point at which there was no risk to the *Amherst* and yet close enough to make frequent trips to

21

the net feasible.

Then, with a work party she jetted out to the net and selected fragments which might be worth examining. The cargo pod was already divided into sections. At first these were all kept in vacuum status at -270° celsius, or 3° absolute. Once back in the *Amherst*, Ni Mor- gana activated the monitors and began one of her legendary forty-hour days.

"I've got a lot of dirty ice," was her initial comment four days later, after she'd had some sleep and a second review of her data. "Most of the stuff has identifiable intrusions, particles of rock and metal, there are also —" There was a long pause. "— some very unusual particles that I have never encountered before. Before anyone gets an idea I don't want to give, there is no evidence of any artifact."

As the science officer held five degrees in different disciplines and had landed on three or four dozen alien surfaces, that was an intriguing admission.

The next morning she suited up again and jetted around the netted debris, looking for her special interest, 'space worms'.

Captain Fargoe had approved Lieutenant Benden's preliminary flight data and Ross continued his study of the EEC survey reports and the two cryptic messages that were the only communications from the colony world.

"IF THERE IS A LIFE FORM," NI Morgana said at her most tentative in the week's officers' meeting, "its response time is far too slow for us to discern. There have been some anomalies both in superconductivity and in cryochemistry that I want to follow up. I shall begin a series of tests, slowly warming some representative samples to see what occurs."

The next week she reported: "At -200° celsius, some of the larger particles are showing relative movement, but whether this is driven by an anomalous internal structure or a reaction to the warmer temperature I cannot as yet ascertain."

"Keep in mind at all times, Lieutenant," the captain said at her sternest, "what happened to the *Roma*!"

"Ma'am, I always do!"

The 'melting of the *Roma*' when the science officer brought aboard a metal-hungry organism was a cautionary example drummed into every science officer.

The following week Ni Morgana was almost jubilant. "Captain, there is a real life form in some of the larger chunks from the cloud. Ovoid shapes, with an exceedingly hard crust of material, they have some liquid, perhaps helium, inside. They're very strange but I'm sure they're not artifacts. I'm bringing one sample up above 0° C this week."

The captain held up an admonishing finger at her science officer. "At all times, keep the *Roma* in mind."

"Ma'am, even the situation on the *Roma* didn't happen in a day."

In the process of leaving the conference room, the captain stopped and stared quizzically at Ni Morgana. "Are you deliberately misquoting something, Lieutenant?"

"MISTER BENDEN!" THE SCIENCE OF-
ficer's peremptory summons over the
com-unit by his ear jolted Ross Vaclav
Benden out of his bunk and to his feet.

"Ma'am?"

"Get down to the lab on the double,
mister!"

Benden struggled into his shipsuit as
he ran down the companionway, stab-
bing feet into soft shipshoes. It was oh-
dark-hundred of the dog watch, for no
one was even in Five Deck's lounge area
as he raced across it and to the appropriate grav shaft down to the lab. He skid-
ded to a halt at the door, skinning his
forearms on the frame as he braked and
fell into the facility. He almost knocked
over Lieutenant Ni Morgana. She
pointed to the observation chamber.

"Funkit, what in the name of the
holies is that?" he wanted to know as his
eyes fell on the writhing grayish pink
and puke yellow mass that oozed and
roiled on the monitor screen. He could
understand why everyone was standing

well back even if the mass was, in reality, ten kilometers from the *Amherst*.

"If that is what fell on Pern," Ni Morgana said, "I don't blame 'em for shrieking for help!"

"Let me through," and the captain, clad in a terry-cloth caftan, had to exert some strength to push pass the mesmerized group watching the phenomenon. "Gods above! What have you unleashed, mister?"

"We're taping the show, ma'am," Ni Morgana said as well as prominently waving the hand she held over the 'destruct' button that would activate laser fire. Benden could see her eyes glittering with clinical fascination. "According to the readings I'm getting, this complex organism exhibits some similarity to Terran mycorrhizoids in its linear structure. But it's enormous! Damn!"

The organism suddenly collapsed in on itself and became a thick viscous inanimate puddle. The science officer tapped out some commands on the waldo keyboard and a unit extruded towards the mass, scooped up a sample in a self-sealing beaker and retreated. Lights glittered on the remote testing apparatus that analyzed the sample.

"What happened to it?" Captain Fargoe demanded and Benden admired how firm her voice was. He was very much aware that he had the shakes.

"I should be able to tell you when the analysis is finished on that sample of the residue but I'd hazard the guess that, with such rapid expansion, if it found no sustenance in the chamber — and there was none apart from a very thin atmosphere — that it died of starvation. That's only a guess."

"But," Benden heard himself saying, "if this is the Pernese organism . . ."

"That's only a possibility at this point," Ni Morgana said quickly. "We must first discover how it managed to get from the cloud to Pern's surface."

"Good point," the captain murmured and Benden was almost angry at her amused tone. There was nothing remotely funny about what they had just witnessed.

"But if it did, and it's what attacked Pern, I can't blame 'em for wanting help," said Ensign Nev, whose complexion was still slightly green.

The captain gave him a long look that caused him to flush from neck to a scalp that was visible under his latest space trim.

"Captain," Ni Morgana said as she pressed the destruct button, destroying the dead organism by laser fire, "I request permission to join the Pern landing party to pursue my investigation of this phenomenon."

"Granted!" The captain paused, stepping over the lintel of the lab with a wicked grin. "I always prefer volunteers for landing parties."

WHOEVER MIGHT HAVE ENVIED Lieutenant Benden the assignment had different feelings once details of the 'organism' became scuttlebutt. A concise report from Lieutenant Ni Morgana was published to quell the more rampant

speculations and her lab team became welcome as experts at any mess.

Ross Vaclav Benden had nightmares about his uncle: the admiral, unexpectedly garbed in dress whites, great purple sash of the Hero of the Cygnus Campaign, and a full assortment of other prestigious and rare decorations on his chest, struggled against engulfment by the monstrosity of the lab chamber. Determined to do his best by his uncle, Ross studied, to the point of perfect recall, the EEC valuation of Pern. The terse all-safe message by Admiral Benden and Governor Boll and Tubberman's mayday were easy to memorize, the latter tantalizingly ambiguous. Why had the colony botanist sent the message? Why not Paul Benden or Emily Boll, or one of the senior section heads?

Although this was not Benden's first landing-party command, he believed in checking and double-checking every aspect of the assignment. Since there might be hostile conditions including omnivorous organisms and other enigmas to be solved or avoided on Pern's surface, Ross Benden judiciously plotted an alternative holding orbit until the escape window opened up for their rendezvous with the *Amherst*. The landing party had five days, three hours, fourteen minutes on the surface to conduct its investigations. To his chagrin, Ni Morgana asked for Ensign Nev as the junior officer.

"He needs some experience, Ross," Ni Morgana said, blandly ignoring Benden's disgruntlement, "and he's had some xeno training. He's strong and he obeys orders even as he's turning green. He's got to learn sometime. Captain Fargoe thinks this could give him valuable experience."

Benden had no option but to accept the inevitable, but he asked for Sergeant Greene to command his marines. That tough burly man knew more about the hazards that could embroil landing parties than Benden ever would. Having seen the organism which Saraidh had unleashed, Ross wanted solid experience to offset Nev's ingenuousness. If

31

that was the proper word for the boy.

"Just what were you like as an ensign, Lieutenant?" Ni Morgana asked, giving him a sly sideways glance.

"I was never that gauche," he replied tartly, which was true enough since he'd been reared in a Service family and had absorbed proper behavior with normal nutrients. Then he relented, grinning wryly back at her as he remembered a few incidents that he hoped she had no access to. "This sounds like a fairly routine mission: find and evaluate."

"Let's hope so," Saraidh replied earnestly.

Ross Benden was, in another sense, delighted to be teamed up with the elegant science officer. She was his senior in years but not in Fleet, for she had done her scientific training before applying to the Service. She was also the only woman aboard who kept her hair long, though it was generally dressed in intricate arrangements of braids. The effect was somehow regal and very feminine: an effect at variance with her expertise

in the various forms of contact sport that were enjoyed in the *Amherst*'s gym complex. If she had made any liaisons on board, they were not general knowledge, though he'd overheard speculation about her tastes. He had always found her agreeable company and a competent officer, though they hadn't shared more than a watch or two until now.

"Did you see the tape of that thing?" Ross Benden heard the nasal voice of Lieutenant Zane saying later as he passed the wardroom. "There'll be no one left alive down there. Ni Morgana has proved the Oort cloud generated that life form so it wasn't of Nastie manufacture. There's no rationale for taking a chance and landing on that planet if any of those things are alive down there! And they could be with an entire planet to eat up."

Benden paused to listen, knowing perfectly well that, despite the dangers involved, Zane would have given a kidney to be in the landing party. Nev was at least an improvement on the sour and

supercilious Zane. And when the navigation officer added some invidious remarks that Benden was only chosen because of his relationship to one of the leaders of the colony, Benden passed quickly down the corridor before his temper got the better of his discretion.

AS THE *AMHERST*'S MAJESTIC PASsage through the system approached the point where the shuttle could be launched, Benden called for a final briefing session.

"We'll spiral down to the planetary surface in a corkscrew orbit which will allow us to examine the northern hemisphere on our way to the site of record on the southern continent at longitude 30°," he said, calling up the flight-path on the big screen in the conference room. "We've landmarks from the original survey of three volcanic cones that ought to be visible from some distance as we make our final approach. Survey report said the soil there would be viable for hardy Earth and Altairian hybrids so it

34

is reasonable to assume that they started their agrarian venture there. The Tubberman mayday came in some nine years after landing so they should have been well entrenched."

"Not enough to avoid that organism," Nev said flatly.

"Your theory would hold water, Ensign," Saraidh said at her mildest, "if I could figure out how the organism transported itself from the Oort cloud to Pern's surface."

"Nasties sowed it in Pern's atmosphere," Nev responded with no hesitation.

"Nasties are more direct in their tactics," the science officer replied with a diffident shrug and turned to Benden with a question.

"We taught 'em to be cautious, Lieutenant," Nev went on. "And devious. And . . ."

"Nev!" Benden called the ensign to order.

Benden kept his expression neutral but he wondered if Ni Morgana was regretting her choice of the irrepressible Nev and his wild theories. If the science officer hadn't found a transport vector for the organism, the Nasties were unlikely to have discovered it. Their forte was metallurgy, not biology. Nev subsided and the briefing continued.

"Once we have made landfall, we may also have answers to that question and others. It is obvious our search must begin at the site of record. We will also have made a good sweep of the entire planetary surface and can deviate if we find traces of human settlements elsewhere. We board the *Erica* at 02:30 tomorrow morning. Any questions?"

"What do we do if the place is swarming with those *things*?" asked Nev, swallowing hard.

"What would you do, Nev?" Benden asked.

"Leave!"

"Tut tut, mister," Ni Morgana said. "How will you ever increase your understanding of xenobiological forms unless you examine closely whatever samples

36

come your way?"

Ensign Nev's eyes bugged out. "Begging your pardon, Lieutenant, but *you're* the science officer."

"Indeed I am," and Ni Morgana rose, the scrape of her chair covering a mutter of gratitude from the end of the table occupied by the four marines assigned to the landing party.

LAUNCHED FROM THE *AMHERST*, the gig proceeded at a smart inner system speed toward the blue pebble in the sky that was Rukbat's third planet. It began to dominate the forward screen, serene and clear, beautiful and innocuous. Benden had plotted the gig's course to intercept the geosynchronous orbit of the three colony ships to see if the colonists had left a message to be retrieved. But when he opened communications, the only response was the standard identification response, stating the name and designation of the *Yokohama*.

"That might not mean anything," Saraidh remarked as Benden looked disappointed. "If the colony's up and running, they won't have much use for these hulks. Though I find that sight rather sad," she added as Rukbat suddenly illuminated the deserted vessels.

"Why?" Nev asked, surprised by her observation.

Saraidh gave a shrug of her slender, elegant shoulders. "Look up their battle records and you might appreciate their present desuetude more."

"Their what?" Nev looked blank.

"Look up that word, too," she said and, in an almost cloying tone, spelled it for him.

"Old sailors never die, they just fade away," Benden murmured, eyes on the three hulks, feeling a constriction in his throat and a slight wetness in his eyes as the gig drifted away from them, leaving them to continue on their ordained path.

"Soldiers, not sailors," Saraidh said, "but the quotation is apt." Then she frowned at a reading on her board. "We've got two beacons registering. One at the site of record and another much further south. Enlarge the southern hemisphere for me, will you, Ross? Along 70° longitude and nearly a twelve hundred klicks from the stronger one." Ross and Saraidh exchanged looks. "Maybe there are survivors! Pretty far south though, over mountain ranges of respectable height. I read altitudes of 2,400 rising to more than 9,000 meters above sea level. We'll land at the site of record first."

AS THE GIG SLANTED IN OVER THE northern pole, it was obvious that this hemisphere was enduring a stormy and bitterly cold winter: most of the land-mass was covered by snow and ice. Instruments detected no source of power or light, and very little heat radiation in areas where humans usually settled, the river valleys, the plains, the shoreline. There was one hiccup of a blip over the large island, just off the coast of the northern hemisphere. The reading was too faint to suggest any significant congregation of settlers. If they had followed the usual multiplication so characteristic of colonies, the population should now be close to the half million mark, even allowing for natural disasters and those mortality patterns normal for a primitive economy.

"We'll do another low level pass if we've time later. The settlers were determined to be agrarian but they might be using fossil fuels," Saraidh said as they plunged toward the equator, leaving the snowclad continent behind them and slanting down across the tropical sea. "Lots of marine life. Some big ones," she added. "Bigger than the survey team reported."

"They took Terran dolphins with them," Nev said. "Mentasynth-enhanced dolphins," he added, as if that altered the fact.

"I don't think rescuing dolphins is what Captain Fargoe has in mind, even if we had the facility to do so," Saraidh said. "Have either of you any training in interspecies' communications? I don't. So, let's table that notion for now."

"There's another consideration. How long do dolphins live?" Ross asked. "Remember, this trouble started when the colony was down eight to nine years. In your report, Lieutenant, you did mention that further tests with the organism proved that water drowned it and organic fire consumed it. Mentasynth-enhanced creatures have good memories, sure. But how many generations of dolphins have there been? Would they even be aware of what happened on land? Much less remember?"

"Would they want to, is more the case," Saraidh said. "They're independent and very intelligent. Clearly they have survived and multiplied from the complement that came with the colony. They'd cut their losses and survive on their own. I would, if I were a dolphin."

Then Saraidh started the recorders on the gig's delta wing to take a record of the plunging antics of the large marine life as the *Erica* swooped over the ocean on their final descent toward the site of record.

41

"Records state that the *Bahrain* brought fifteen female dolphins and nine males," Nev said suddenly. "Dolphins reproduce — what? Once a year. There could be nearly eight hundred of 'em in the seas right now. That's a lot of terrestrial life forms we'd be abandoning."

"Abandoning? Hell, Cahill, they're in their element. Look at them, they're doing their damnedest to keep pace with us."

"Maybe they have a message for us," Nev went on earnestly.

"We look for humans first, Ensign," the science officer said firmly. "Then we'll check the dolphins! Ross, I'm not getting anything from the ship-to-ground interface that's recorded for the site. It's inoperative, too."

"Now hear this! Buckle up for landing," Ross said, opening a channel to the marines' quarters.

"Mullah!" was Saraidh's awed comment as they saw the two ruined volcanic craters and the smoking cone of the third.

Ross could say nothing, appalled by

the extent of the eruption. He'd expected nothing so catastrophic as this. Or had this devastation occurred after the organism had begun to fall? While he had more or less resigned himself that he was unlikely to encounter his uncle, he had hoped to chat with the admiral's descendants. He certainly hadn't anticipated this level of devastation. They flew over the landing field tower, its beacon now blinking, activated by the proximity of the gig.

"See those mounds, just coming up on portside?" Saraidh pointed. "They've got the outlines of shuttles. How many did the colonists have?"

"Records say six," Nev replied. "*Bahrain* had one, *Buenos Aires* two and the *Yoko* three. Plus a captain's gig."

"Only three parked there now. Wonder where the others went."

"Maybe they were used to get out of this place when the volcano blew?"

"But where to? There were no signs of human habitation on the northern continent," Benden said, sternly re-

43

pressing his dismay.

Saraidh let out a thin high whistle. "And those other regular mounds are — were — the settlement. Neatly, if not aesthetically, laid out. Must have built well, for nothing seems to have collapsed from the weight of ash and dirt. Lava's cooled. Ross, got a reading of how deep that ash is over the ground?"

"We do indeed, Saraidh," Ross replied with relief. "A metallic grid is present a half meter below the surface. No problem landing — it'll be nice and soft."

Which it was. While waiting for the disturbed ash to settle, both officers and marines suited up, checking masks, breathing tanks, and strapping on lift belts. These would convey them safely above the ash to the settlement.

"What're those?" one of the marines asked as the landing party assembled to hover a meter above the ash-coated ground outside the *Erica*. He pointed to a series of long semicircular mounds, bulging up out of the ash. "Tunnels?"

44

"Unlikely. Not big enough and don't seem to go anywhere," Ni Morgana said, deftly manipulating her altitude and forward jets. She hovered to one side of the nearest mound and pushed with her foot. It collapsed with a dusty implosion and a stench that the filters of their masks worked hard to neutralize. "Faugh! Dead organism. Now, why didn't that puddle?" She took out a specimen tube and carefully gathered some of the residue, sealing it and putting that tube in a second padded container.

"It fed on ash or grass or something?" asked Ensign Nev.

"We'll check that out later. Let's look at the buildings. Scag, stay by the gig," Benden ordered one of the marines. And then gestured for the others to follow him up to the empty settlement.

"Not empty," Ross said an hour later, increasingly more pessimistic about finding any survivors. Contact with a cousin or two would be something to write home about. So he clutched at a vain hope. "Emptied. They didn't leave a thing they could use. Nasties would have obliterated any trace of humans."

"That's true enough," Saraidh said. "And there's no evidence of Nasties at all. Merely an evacuated settlement. There is that second beacon to the southwest. There's certainly nothing here to give us any explanations. Your point about everything being emptied is well taken, Benden. They closed shop here, but that doesn't mean they didn't open it up elsewhere."

"Using the three missing shuttles," Nev added brightly.

Airborne again in the *Erica*, heading directly toward the beacon, they overpassed the rest of the settlement, taping the one smoking volcano crater and the melted structures below it. No sooner were they over the river than the landscape showed another form of devastation.

The prevailing winds had minimized the dispersal of volcanic dust but oddly

47

enough, there were only occasional stands of vegetation and large circles of parched soil.

"Like something had sprinkled the land with whopping great acid drops," Cahill Nev said, awed at the extent of the markings.

"Not acid. No way," Benden replied. He keyed the relevant section of the report he knew so well. "The EEC survey team found similar circular patches, and they also reported that botanical succession had started."

"It has to be the Oort organism," Nev said enthusiastically. "On the cruiser it died of starvation. It had plenty to eat here."

"The organism has to get here first, mister," Ni Morgana said bitingly. "And we haven't established how it could cross some 600 million miles of space to drop on Pern." Ross, glancing at her set expression, thought she was rapidly considering improbable transport media. "Terrain's flat enough here, Mister Benden," she went on. "Try a low level pass and give us a closer look at that . . . that diseased ground.''

Benden obliged, noting once again how responsive the *Erica* was to the helm, smoothly skimming the often uneven terrain. Not that he expected something to pop up out of those polka dots, but you never knew on alien worlds. Even ones thoroughly surveyed by Exploration and Evaluation teams. They might not have found any predators but something dangerous had put in an appearance nine years after the settlers took hold. And the Tubberman appeal hadn't mentioned a volcanic eruption.

Klick after klick they passed over circles and overlapping circles and triple circles. Ni Morgana remarked that some succession was visible on their peripheries. She asked Benden to land so she could take more samples, including clods of the regenerating vegetation. Across a broad river there were swaths of totally unharmed trees and acres of broad-leafed and unscathed vegetation. Over one wide pasture they caught sight of a cloud of dust, but whatever stirred it disappeared under the broad leaves of a thick forest. They spotted no trace of human habitation. Not even a dirt-covered mound that might be the remains of a building or a wall.

The second beacon signal became stronger as they neared the foothills of a great barrier of mountains, snow-clad even in what must be high summer in this hemisphere. Gradually the pips altered from rhythmic bleeps to a sustained note as they homed in on the beacon.

"There's nothing here but a sheer cliff," Ross said, disgusted as he let the gig hover over the destination, the single note exacerbating his nerves.

"That may well be, Ross," Saraidh said, "but I'm getting body-heat readings."

Nev pointed excitedly. "That plateau below us is too level to be natural. And there are terraces below it. See? And what about that path down into the valley? And hey, this cliff has windows!"

"And is definitely inhabited!" exclaimed Saraidh, pointing to starboard where a doorway appeared in the cliff face. "Put her down, Ross!"

BY THE TIME THE *ERICA* HAD SETtled to the smoothed surface, a file of people came running down the plateau towards it: their cries, audible from the exterior speakers, were of hysterical welcome. They ranged in age from early twenties to late forties. Except for a white-haired man, his mane trimmed to shoulder length, whose lined face and slow movements suggested a person well into his eighth or ninth decade. His emergence halted the demonstrations and the others stood aside to allow him a clear passage to the gig's portal where he halted.

"The patriarch," Saraidh murmured, straightening her tunic and settling her beaked cap straight on top of her braids.

"Patriarch?" Nev asked.

"Look it up later — if the term is not self-explanatory," Benden shot at him over his shoulder, operating the airlock release. He glanced warningly at the

51

marines who replaced their drawn hand
weapons. As soon as the airlock swung
open and the ramp extruded, the small
crowd was silent. All eyes turned to the
old man who pulled himself even more
erect, a patronizing smile on his weath-
ered face.

"You finally got here!"

"A message was received at Federated headquarters," Ross Benden began,
"signed by a Theodore Tubberman. Are
you he?"

The man gave a snort of disgust.
"I'm Stev Kimmer," and he flicked one
hand to his brow in a jaunty parody of a
proper Fleet salute. "Tubberman's long
dead. I designed that capsule, by the
way."

"You did well," Benden replied. In-
explicably, Benden suddenly did not
care to identify himself. So he introduced Saraidh Ni Morgana and Ensign
Nev. "But why did you send that capsule to Federation headquarters, Kimmer?"

"That wasn't my idea. Ted Tubberman insisted." Kimmer shrugged. "He paid me for my work, not my advice. As it is, you've taken nearly too damned long to get here." He scowled with irritation.

"The *Amherst* is the first vessel to enter the Sagittarian Sector since the message was received." Saraidh Ni Morgana said, unruffled by his criticism. She had noted that Ross had not given his name. She hoped that Ensign Nev had also noted the omission. "We've just come from the site on record."

"No one came back to Landing, then?" Kimmer demanded. Benden thought his habit of interrupting Fleet officers could become irritating. "With Thread gone, that'd be the place they'd return to. The ground-to-ship interface's there."

"The interface is inoperative," Benden said, carefully neutral as the old man's arrogance grated on him.

"Then the others are dead," Kimmer stated flatly. "Thread got 'em all!"

"Thread?"

"Yes, Thread." Kimmer's palpable

anger was tinged with deep primal emotions, not the least of which was a healthy fear. "That's what they named the organism that attacked the planet. Because it fell from the skies like a rain of deadly thread, consuming all it touched, animal, man, and vegetable. We burned it out of the skies, on the ground, day after fucking day. And still it came. We're all that's left. Eleven of us and we only survived because we have a mountain above us and we hoarded our supplies, waiting for help to come."

"Are you positive that you're the sole survivors?" Ni Morgana asked. "Surely you were settled in the eight or nine years you had before this menace attacked you."

"Before Thread fell, the population was close to twenty thousand, but we're all that's left," Kimmer said, now defiant. "And you cut it mighty fine getting here. I couldn't risk another generation with such a small gene pool."

Then one of the women, who bore a strong resemblance to Kimmer, tugged

at his arm. And he made a grimace that could be taken for a smile. "My daughter reminds me that this is a poor welcome for our long awaited rescuers. Come this way. I've something laid by in the hope of this day."

Lieutenant Benden gestured for two marines to remain on board before he followed Ni Morgana down the ramp, Nev treading on his heels in his eagerness.

The silence which had held Kimmer's small group while he had addressed the spacemen relaxed now into gestures and smiles of welcome. But Benden took note of the tenseness of the oldest three men. They stood just that much apart from the women and youngsters to suggest they distanced themselves deliberately. They had a distinctly Asian cast of countenance, jet black hair trimmed neatly to their earlobes: they were lean and looked physically fit. The oldest woman, who bore a strong resemblance to the three men, walked just a step behind Kimmer in a manner that suggested subservience: an attitude which Benden found distasteful as he and his party followed them to the entrance.

The three younger women were ethnic mixes in feature, though one had brown hair. All were slender and graceful as they tried to contain their excitement. They whispered to each other, casting glances back at Greene and the other marine. At a brusque order from Kimmer, they ran on ahead, into the cliff. The three youngest, two boys and a girl, showed the mixing of ethnic groups more than their elders. Benden wondered just how close the blood bonding was. Kimmer would not have been fool enough to sire children on his own daughters?

Exclamations of surprise were forced from each of the three officers as they entered a spacious room with a high, vaulted ceiling; a room nearly as big as the gig's on-ship hangar. Nev gawked like any off-world stupe while Ni Morgana's expression was of delighted ap-

preciation. This was clearly the main living space of the cliff dwelling for it had been broken up into distinct areas for work, study, dining, and handicrafts. The furnishings were made of a variety of materials, including extruded plastic in bright hard colors. The walls were well hung with curious animal furs and hand-loomed rugs of unusual design. Above those and all along the upper wall space, a vivid panorama had been drawn: first of stylized figures standing or sitting before what were clearly monitors and keyboards. Other panels showed figures who plowed and planted fields or tended animals of all sorts; panels which led around to the innermost wall that was decorated by scenes Benden knew too well, the cities of Earth and Altair and three spaceships with unfamiliar constellations behind them. At the apex of the ceiling vault was the Rukbat system, and one planet that was shown to have a highly elliptical, and possibly an erratic orbit from slightly beyond the Oort cloud to an

aphelion below Pern's.

Ni Morgana nudged Benden in the ribs and said in a barely audible whisper. "Unlikely as it seems, I've just figured out one way the Oort organisms might have reached Pern. I'll be damned sure of my theory before I mention it."

"The murals," Kimmer was saying in a loud and proprietary voice, "were to remind us of our origins."

"Did you have stone-cutters?" Nev asked abruptly, running his hand over the glassy smooth walls.

One of the older black-haired men stepped forward. "My parents, Kenjo and Ito Fusaiyuki, designed and carved all the principal rooms. I am Shensu. These are my brothers, Jiro and Kimo: our sister, Chio." He gestured to the woman who was reverently withdrawing a bottle from a shelf in a long dresser.

With a searing glance at Shensu, Kimmer hastily took the initiative again. "These are my daughters, Faith and Hope. Charity is setting out the glasses." Then with a flick of his fingers, he indicated Shensu. "You may introduce my grandchildren."

"Pompous old goat," muttered Ni Morgana to Benden but she smiled as the grandchildren were introduced as Meishun, Alun and Pat, the two boys being in their mid-teens.

"This Stake could have supported many more families if only those who had said they'd join us had kept their promises," Kimmer went on bitterly. Then with an imperious gesture, he waved the guests to come to the table and be served of the wine he was pouring: a rich fruity red.

"Well come, men and women of the *Amherst*!" was Kimmer's toast and he touched glasses with each of them.

Benden noticed, as Ni Morgana did, that the others were served a paler red by Meishun. Watered, Benden thought. They could at least be equal to us, today of all days! Shensu hid his resentment better than his two brothers did. The women seemed not to notice for they passed dishes of cheese bits and tasty small crackers to everyone. Then Kimmer gestured for the guests to be seated. Benden gave a discreet hand signal to the two marines who took the end seats at the long table and remained watchful, taking only small sips of the celebratory wine.

"Where to start?" Kimmer began, setting his wine glass down deliberately.

"The beginning," Ross Benden said wryly, hoping that he might learn what had happened to his uncle before disclosing his identity. There was something about Kimmer — not his anger nor his autocratic manner — that Benden instinctively distrusted. But perhaps a man who had managed to survive in a hostile environment had the right to a few peculiarities.

"Of the end?" And Kimmer's spiteful expression served to increase Benden's dislike.

"If that is when you and the botanist Tubberman sent that homing device," Benden replied, encouragingly.

"It was and our position was then

hopeless, though few were realists enough to admit it, especially Benden and Boll."

"Could you have got back up to the colony ships then?" Ni Morgana asked, nudging Ross Benden when she felt him stir angrily.

"No way," and Kimmer snorted with disgust. "They used what fuel the gig had left to send Fusaiyuki up to reconnoiter. They thought they might be able to divert whatever it was that brought the Thread. That was before they realized that the wanderer planet had dragged in a tail that would shower this wretched planet with Thread for fifty frigging years. And if that wasn't bad enough, they let Avril steal the gig and that was the end of any chance we had of sending someone competent for help." The recital of that forty-year-old memory agitated Kimmer, and his face became suffused with red.

"It was definitely established that the organism had been carried from the Oort cloud?" Ni Morgana asked, her usually

63

calm voice edged with excitement.

Kimmer gave her a quelling glance. "In the end that was all they discovered despite their waste of fuel and manpower."

"There were only three shuttles left at the landing site. Do you suppose some people managed to escape in them?" said Ni Morgana in a deliberately soothing tone. Benden could see the glitter of her eyes as she sipped calmly at her wine.

Kimmer glared at her with contempt. "Where could they escape to? There was no fuel left! And power-packs for sleds and skimmers were in short supply."

"Barring the lack of fuel, were the shuttles still operational?"

"I said, there was no fuel. No fuel!" and he banged his fist on the table. Benden, looking away from the man's deep bitterness noted the faint look of amusement on Shensu's face.

"There was no fuel," Kimmer repeated with less vehemence. "The shuttles were so much scrap without fuel. So

I haven't any idea why there'd be only three shuttles at Landing. I left the settlement shortly after the bitch blew the gig up." He glared impartially at the *Amherst* officers. "I had every right to leave then, to establish a Stake and do what I could to preserve my own skin. Anyone with any sense, charterer or contracter, should have done the same. Maybe they did. Holed up to wait out the fifty years. Or, maybe they sailed away into the rising sun. They had ships, you know. Yes, that's it. Old Jim Tillek sailed them out of Monaco Bay into the rising sun." He gave a bark of harsh laughter.

"They went west?" Benden asked.

Kimmer favored him with a contemptuous glance and made a wild gesture with one arm. "How the hell would I know? I wasn't anywhere near the place."

"And you settled here," Ni Morgana asked blandly, "in the dwelling built by Kenjo and Ito Fusaiyuki."

Her phrasing was, Benden thought,

a little unfortunate for the question angered Kimmer even more. The veins in his temples stood out and his face contorted.

"Yes, I settled here when Ito begged me to stay. Kenjo was dead. Avril killed him to get the gig. Ito'd had a difficult birth with Chio and their kids were too young to be useful then. So Ito asked me to take over." Someone's breath hissed on intake and Kimmer glared at the three sons, unable to spot the culprit. "You'd all have died without me!" he said in a flat but somehow cautionary tone.

"Most assuredly," Shensu said, his surface courtesy not quite masking a deep resentment.

"You have survived, haven't you? And my beacon brought us help, didn't it!" Kimmer banged on the table with both fists and sprang to his feet. "Admit it! My homer and my beacon have brought us rescue."

"They did indeed lead us to you, Mr. Kimmer," Benden said in a tone he barefacedly borrowed from Captain Fargoe

66

when she was dressing down an insubordinate rating. "However, my orders are to search and discover any and all survivors on this planet. You may not be the only ones."

"Oh yes, we are. By all the gods, we're the only ones," Kimmer said, with an edge of panic in his voice. "And you can't leave us here!" His eyes turned a bit wild.

"What the lieutenant means, Mr. Kimmer," Ni Morgana put in soothingly, "is that our orders are to search for any other survivors."

"No one else survives," Kimmer said in a flat, toneless voice. "I can assure you that." He spashed wine into his glass and drank half of it, wiping his mouth with a trembling hand.

Because Ross Benden was not looking at the old man just then but at the three brothers seated across the table, he caught the glitter in the eyes of Shensu and Jiro. He waited for them to speak up but they remained silent and inscrutable. Palpably they had knowledge that they would not communicate to their rescuers in front of Stev Kimmer. Well, Benden would see them privately later. Meanwhile, Kimmer was coming across as a somewhat unreliable opportunist. He might assert that he had the right to set off and establish a Stake when the colony was obviously in terrible straits but, to Benden, it sounded more as if Kimmer had fled in a craven fashion. Was it just luck that he had known where to find Ito, and this Kenjo's Stake?

"My sled had a powerful com-unit," Kimmer went on, revived by the wine, "and once I'd erected the beacon on the plateau here, I listened in to what was broadcast. Not that there was anything important beyond where the next Fall was. How many power-packs had been recharged. If they had enough sleds able to cover the next Fall. A lot of the Stake-holders had come back to Landing by then, centralizing resources. Then, after the volcanoes blew, I heard their messages as they scurried away from Landing. There was a lot of static interference

and transmissions got so fragmented that I couldn't hear most of what was said. They were frantic, I can tell you, by the time they abandoned Landing. Then the signals got too weak for me to pick up. I never did find out where they planned to go. It might have been west. It might have been east.

"Oh," and he waved one hand helplessly, "I tried when the last signal died. I only had one full power pack left by then. I couldn't waste that in futile searches, now could I? I'd Ito and four small kids. Then Ito got so ill, I went back to Landing to see if they'd left any medicines behind. But Landing was covered in ash and lava, great rivers of it, hot and glowing. Damned near singed the plastic off the hull.

"I checked all the stations on the lower Jordan. Paradise River, Malay, even Boca where Benden lived. No one. Fierce waste of material, though, piled as storm-wrack along the coast at one point. Looked to me as if they'd lost the cargo ships in a storm. We got bad ones blowing in from the sea — or maybe the aftermath of a tsunami. We had one of those after some sea volcano blew up to the east somewhere. Missed us though on Bitkim Island.

"Last message I ever heard, and only parts of it at that, was Benden telling everyone to conserve power, stay inside, and just let that frigging Thread fall. I guess it got him, too."

Ni Morgana's thigh deliberately pressed against Benden's and he took it as sympathy. Though the old man's rambling had been confused and sometimes he contradicted himself, his statement had the ring of truth as he sat silently contemplating his wine glass. Then he roused, raising a finger to bring Chio to his side. She refilled his glass. Then, with an apologetic smile, she offered wine to the other guests whose glasses were barely touched. Down the table from Kimmer, the three brothers sat very close together, saying little but looking with a thinly veiled hatred of Kimmer.

"We had eight good years on Pern before disaster struck," Kimmer was saying now, casting further back in his memory. "I heard that Benden and Boll swore blind that they could lick Thread. Except for Ted Tubberman and a few others, they had half the colony behind them, too entranced by the great reputations of the admiral and the governor," and the titles were pronounced disparagingly, "to believe they could fail. Tubberman wanted to send for help then. The colony voted the motion down.

"Where we were on Bitkim Island, we didn't get much Thread but I heard what it did: wiped out whole Stakes down to the metal they'd been wearing. Ate anything, Thread did, gorged until it blew up too fast to live; but it could burrow down and the next generation would begin. Fire stopped it, and metal. It drowned in water. The fish, even the dolphins, thrived on it, or so the dolphineers said. Humph. Damned stuff only let up a couple a years back. Otherwise, we've had this frigging menace raining down on us every ten days or so for fifty fucking years."

"You did well to survive, Mr. Kimmer," Saraidh said in a flattering purr as she leaned forward to elicit more confidences, "for fifty long years. But how? It must have taken tremendous effort."

"Kenjo'd started 'ponics. Had some sense, that man, even with this fanatic thing he had about flying and being in the air. Space crazy he was. But I was better at contrapting the things you need to live. I taught this whole bunch everything I knew — not that they're grateful to me," and his spiteful eyes rested on the three Fusaiyukis. "We saved horses, sheep, cattle, chickens before Thread could ooze all over 'em. I'd salvaged one of the old grass-makers they used the first year, before they'd planted Earth grass and that Altair hybrid got started." He paused, narrowing his eyes. "Tubberman had another type of grass growing before they shunned him. I'd none of that seed but enough to keep us going

72

until we could plant out again. As long as I had power packs, I foraged and saved every scrap I could find. So we survived, and survived real good."

"Then others could have, too?" Saraidh asked mildly.

"*No!*" thundered Kimmer, banging the table to emphasize that denial. "No one survived but us. You don't believe me? Tell her, Shensu."

As if making up his mind to obey, Shensu regarded first Kimmer and then the three officers. Then he shrugged.

"After Thread had stopped for three months, Kimmer sent us out to see if anyone lived. We went from the Jordan River west to the Great Desert. We did see long-overgrown ruins where Stakes had been started. We saw many domestic animals. I was surprised to see how many animals had managed to survive for we saw much devastation of fertile land. We traveled for eight months. We saw no one human nor any evidence of human endeavor. We returned to our hold." He shot a single challenging look

at Kimmer before his expression settled into its mask.

Benden had a stray thought — Kimmer had sent them out, not to search for survivors, but hoping they wouldn't return.

"We're miners, too," Shensu continued unexpectedly. Kimmer sat up, too enraged at the bland disclosure to form words. Shensu smiled at that reaction. "We have mined, ores and gemstones, as soon as we were strong enough to wield pick and shovel. All of us, my half sisters, and our children, too. Kimmer taught us how to cut gems. He insisted that we be rich enough to pay our way back to civilized worlds."

"You fools! You utter fools! You shouldn't have told them. They'll kill us and take it all. All of it."

"They are Fleet officers, Kimmer," Shensu said, bowing politely to Benden, Ni Morgana, and the astonished Nev. "Like Admiral Benden," and his eyes slid and held Ross Benden's briefly. "They would not be so basely motivated as to

74

steal our fortunes and abandon us. Their orders are to rescue any survivors."

"You will rescue us, won't you?" Kimmer cried, suddenly a terrified old man. "You *must* take us with you. You must!" and now he embarrassed Benden by beginning to blubber. "You must, you must," he kept on insisting, pulling himself toward Benden to grab his tunic.

"Stev, you will make yourself ill again," Chio said, coming to disentangle the grasping hands from Benden's clothing. Her eyes looked her abject apologies for an old man's weakness and her plea for reassurance. The other women fastened apprehensive eyes on the Fleet party.

"Our orders are to establish contact with the survivors — " Benden began, taking refuge in that protocol.

"Lieutenant," Nev intervened, his face contorted with anxiety, "We'd have a weight problem, taking eleven more aboard the *Erica*."

Kimmer moaned.

"We'll discuss this later, Ensign,"

Benden said sharply. Trust Nev to be loose-jawed. "It is time to change the watch." He gave Nev a quelling look and gestured for Greene to accompany him. Greene looked disgusted as he fell in behind the chastened ensign, who was flushed as he realized how badly he had erred.

As Kimmer kept on sobbing "you must take me, you must take me," Benden turned to Shensu and his brothers.

"We do have orders to follow, but I assure you that if we find no other survivors to make your continued residence viable, you will either come with us on the *Erica* or another means will be found to rescue you."

"I appreciate your constraints and your devotion to duty," Shensu said, his composure in marked contrast to Kimmer's collapse. He made a slight bow from the hips. "However," and his face lightened with the slightest of smiles, "my brothers and I have already searched all the old Stakes without success. Will you not accept our investigations as conclusive?" His dignified entreaty was far harder to ignore than Kimmer's blubbering.

Benden tried to assume a noncommittal pose. "I will certainly take that into consideration, Shensu." He was also trying to calculate just how to accommodate eleven extra bodies on the *Erica*. He'd three quarters of a tank; if they stripped unessential equipment, would that still give him enough fuel to lift and a reserve if last minute adjustments were needed in the slingshot maneuver? Damn Nev. His orders were for search only: not rescue. One thing was certain, he trusted Shensu far more than he did Kimmer.

"This mission has another goal, Mr. Fusaiyuki," Ni Morgana said, "if, under these trying circumstances, you could find your way clear to assist us?"

"Certainly. If I can," and Shensu executed a second dignified bow to her.

"Would you have any documentation that Thread comes from the stray planet as Mr. Kimmer intimated?" she asked, pointing to the ceiling and the system diagram. "Or was that only a theory?"

"A theory which my father proved to his satisfaction at least, for he flew up into the stratosphere and observed the debris which the stray planet had dislodged from the Oort cloud and drawn into this part of the system. He had noticed the cloud on his way through the system. I remember him telling me that he would have paid far closer attention had he any idea of the threat it would pose." Shensu's well formed lips curled in a wry smile. "The EEC report evidently gave the erratic planet only a mention. I have my father's notes."

"I'd like to see them," Saraidh said, her voice edged with excitement. "Bizarre as it is," she said to Benden, "it is plausible and unique. Of course, this erratic planet could be a large asteroid, even a comet. Its orbit is certainly a cometary."

"No," Benden replied, shaking his head, "the EEC report definitely identifies it as a planet, though probably a wanderer drawn into Rukbat's family only recently. It orbits across the ecliptic."

"Our father was too experienced an airman to make a mistake." Jiro spoke for the first time, his voice as impassioned as Shensu's was cold. "He was a trained pilot and observed critically and objectively on those missions. We have notes of thanks from Admiral Benden, Governor Boll, and Captain Keroon, all expressing gratitude for his investigation and his selfless dedication to duty." Jiro shot a contemptuous look at Kimmer who was still sobbing, his face pillowed in his arms while Chio tried to comfort and reassure him. "Our father died to discover such truths."

Saraidh murmured something appropriate. "If you would cooperate, further information about this phenomenon would be invaluable."

"Why?" Shensu asked bluntly. "There can't be other worlds that are infested with this menace, can there?"

"Not that we know of, Mr. Fusaiyuki, but all information is valuable to
someone. My orders were to find out
more about this organism."

Shensu shrugged. "You're too late by
several years to do the most valuable
observations," he said with a wry note
in his voice.

"We saw some . . ." Saraidh fumbled
for an exact description of the 'tunnels'
they had seen at Landing, "remnants,
dead shells of these Thread. Would there
be any near you that I could examine?"

Shensu shrugged again. "Some on
the plains below us."

"How far in terms of time?" Saraidh
asked.

"A day's journey."

"Will you guide me?"

"You?" Shensu was surprised.

"Lieutenant Ni Morgana is the science officer of the *Amherst*," Benden put
in firmly. "You will want to assist her in
this investigation, Mr. Fusaiyuki."

Shensu made a small gesture of obe-
dience with his hands.

"Jiro, Kimo," Chio spoke up. Kimmer seemed to have subsided into sleep. "Help me carry him to his room."

The two men rose, their faces blank of expression and picked him up, much as they would a sack, and carried him toward a curtained arch through which they disappeared, Chio following anxiously.

"I'll check on Nev," Benden said, rising, "while you arrange tomorrow's expedition with Shensu, Lieutenant."

"A good idea, Lieutenant."

Benden motioned for the two marines to remain as he made his way out of the superb room, his eyes on the gorgeous murals and their story of mankind's triumph over tremendous odds.

"I COULD WISH, ENSIGN NEV, THAT you would learn to think before you speak," Benden said sternly to the chagrined junior when he returned to the *Erica*.

"I'm real sorry, Lieutenant," and Nev's face was twisted with anxiety,

81

"but we can't just leave them, can we? Not if we can actually rescue them?"

"You've made such calculations?"

"Aye, sir, I did, as soon as I got back on board," and eagerly Nev brought his figures up on the monitor. "Of course, I could only estimate their weight but they can't weigh *that* much and the inward journey only took a quarter of our fuel."

"We've a planet to search, mister," Benden said sharply as he bent to study the figures. This was going to be a command decision on his part: to abandon the search on the basis of the opinion of a few local witnesses or to carry out his original orders scrupulously.

"We weren't expected to *find* survivors, were we?" Nev asked in a tentative voice.

Benden frowned at him. "What exactly do you mean by that, mister?"

"Well, Lieutenant, if Captain Fargoe had expected there'd be survivors, wouldn't she have ordered a troop shuttle? They'd carry a couple of hundred people."

Benden regarded Nev with exasperation. "You know our orders as well as I do: to discover the survivors and their present circumstances. Nothing was intimated that we wouldn't find survivors. Or that we wouldn't find them able to continue their colonial effort."

"But this lot couldn't, could they? There aren't enough of them. I don't trust the old man, but that Shensu's okay."

"When I need your opinion, mister, I'll ask for it," Benden said curtly. Nev subsided to glum silence while Benden continued to peer at the numbers on the screen, half-wishing they would cabalistically rearrange themselves into a solution for his dilemma.

"Establish how much we'd need to jettison, mister, without seriously affecting safety during slingshot. Ascertain just where we can put eleven passengers, and take into your weight consideration the extra padding and harness we'd need to secure them during lift-off."

"Aye, aye, sir." Nev's enthusiasm and the admiring look he gave Benden was almost harder to endure than his chastened funk.

Benden strode to the airlock and out of the ship, taking the crisp air into his lungs as if that would aid his thinking. In a sense Nev was right: the captain hadn't expected that they would find survivors in need of rescue. She had assumed that either the settlers had overcome the disaster or had all succumbed to it. However, these eleven could not, in the name of humanity, be left behind on the planet.

The *Erica*'s remaining fuel would barely accomplish that rescue. It certainly wouldn't allow the Pernese to bring anything back with them to start again elsewhere, like metal ores. Possibly some of those gemstones Shensu had mentioned could be permitted. With no more than the usual shipwreck allowance, these people would be seriously handicapped in the high tech societies on most of the Federation planets and financially unable to establish them-selves in an agrarian economy. They had to have *something*.

If Kimmer could be believed, and it was possible with the estranged brothers corroborating his statements, then these eleven constituted all that remained of the original colonial complement, and further search would be fruitless as well as a waste of fuel that could, really, be put to better use. Did the brothers have any reason to lie? Not, Benden thought, when they hated Kimmer so much. Ah, but they'd want to leave this place, wouldn't they, even if it meant perjuring themselves!

Unusual noises attracted his atten-tion and he walked to the edge of the plateau to check. Some twenty meters below him he saw four people, Jiro and the three youngest, mounted on Earth-type horses, herding a variety of four-legged domestic beasts through a huge aperture in the cliff. He heard an odd call and saw a brown, winged shape hurtling after them. As he watched, a heavy metal door swung on well oiled hinges to close off the opening. The evening breeze, for the light was beginning to fail now on their first day of their five on this planet, wafted some curious smells up to him. He sneezed as he made his way across the plateau to the door to this unusual residence. They'd have to turn those animals loose. Bloody sure, there was no room on board the *Erica* for that mob.

When Benden re-entered the big room, he spotted Ni Morgana and Shensu poring over maps on a smaller table to the left of the main entrance. There were cases of tapes and other paraphernalia along that section of the smooth carved wall.

"Lieutenant, we've got both the original survey maps here and those that the colonists filled in with detailed explorations," Saraidh called to him. "A crying shame this endeavor was so brutally short-lived. They'd a lovely situation here. See," and her scripto touched first one, then another of the shaded areas on the map of the southern continent, "fertile farms producing everything they needed before disaster struck, a viable fishing industry, mines with on-site smelting and manufacturing. And then — " She gave an eloquent shrug.

"Admiral Benden rose to the challenge magnificently," Shensu said, the glow in his eyes altering his whole appearance, making him a far more likeable person. "He called for centralization of all materials and skills. My father commanded the aerial defense. He had flame-throwers mounted on sleds, two forward and one aft, and developed flight patterns that would cover the largest area and destroy quantities of airborne Thread. Ground crews were organized with portable flamers to incinerate what did get through to the ground, before it could burrow and reproduce itself. It was a most valiant effort!"

There was an excitement and a ring in Shensu's voice that made Benden's pulse quicken — he could see that Saraidh was also affected. Shensu's whole attitude was suffused with reverence and awe.

"We were just young boys, but our father came as often as he could and told us what was happening. He was always in touch with our mother. He even spoke to her just before . . . before that final mission." All the animation left Shensu and his expression assumed its habitual taciturnity. "He was brutally murdered just when he might have made the discovery which would have ended Threadfall and preserved the whole colony."

"By this Avril person?" Saraidh asked gently.

Shensu nodded once, his features set. "Then Kimmer came!"

"And now we have come," Saraidh said, pausing a moment before continuing on a brisker note, "and we must somehow gather as much evidence after the fact as possible. There have been many theories about Oort clouds and what they contain. This is the first opportunity to examine such a space-evolved creature, and the disaster it causes on an uninhabited planet. You said the organism burrowed into the ground and reproduced itself? I'd like to see the later stage of the organism's life cycle. Can you show me where?" she asked, looking exceedingly attractive, Benden thought, in her eagerness.

Shensu looked disgusted. "You wouldn't want to see any stage of its life cycle. My mother said that there was only the hunger of it. Which no one should encounter."

"Any sort of residue would aid the research," she said, reaching out to touch his arm. "We need your help, Shensu."

"We needed yours a long time ago," he said in a voice so bitter that Saraidh withdrew her hand, flushing.

"This expedition was mounted as soon as your message came up on the records, Shensu. The delay is not ours," Benden replied crisply. "But we are here now and we'd like your cooperation."

Shensu gave a cynical snort. "Does my cooperation guarantee escape from this place?"

Benden looked him squarely in the eye. "I could not, in conscience, leave you here," he said, having in that moment made his decision, "especially in view of the fact that I also cannot assure you that you would be relieved by another vessel in the near future. I shall however need to have the exact body weights of everyone, and frankly we'll have to strip the *Erica* to accommodate you."

Shensu kept eye contact, his own reaction to Benden's decision unreadable. Benden was aware of Ni Morgana's discreet approval. "Your ship is low on fuel?"

"If we are to successfully lift additional passengers, yes."

"If you did not have to strip the *Erica* to compensate for our weight?" Shensu seemed amused as he watched Benden's reaction. "If you had, say, a full tank, could you allow us to bring enough valuables to assist us to resettle somewhere? Rescue to a pauper's existence would be no rescue at all.''

Benden nodded in acknowledgment of that fact even as he spoke. "Kimmer said there was no more fuel. He was emphatic about it.''

Shensu leaned his body across the table and spoke in a scarcely audible whisper, his black eyes glittering with what Benden read as quiet satisfaction. ''Kimmer doesn't know everything, Lieutenant,'' and now Shensu chuckled, ''though he thinks he does.''

"What do you know that Kimmer doesn't?'' Benden asked, lowering his own voice.

"Spaceship fuel has not changed in the past six decades, has it?'' Shensu asked in his whisper.

"Not for ships of the *Amherst*'s and the *Yoko*'s class,'' Saraidh replied, quietly eager.

"Since you're so interested,'' Shensu said in a conversational voice level as he rose from the table, ''I'd be happy to show you the rest of the Hold. We have a place for everything. I think my es-

91

teemed father had visions of founding a dynasty. My mother said that had not Thread come, there were others of our ethnic type who would have joined them here in Honshu.'' Shensu led them towards a hanging which he pushed aside, gesturing them to proceed through the archway. "They accomplished much before Thread fell.''

He let the hanging fall and joined Saraidh and Benden on the small square landing where stone-cut steps spiraled in both directions. Shensu gestured that they were to ascend.

Saraidh started up. "Wow! This is some staircase,'' she said, as she made the first turn.

"I must warn you that the living room has peculiarities — one of which is an echo effect,'' Shensu said. "Conversations can be overheard in the passages outside. I don't believe *he* has yet recovered from his — disability — but Chio, or one of his daughters, is always eavesdropping for him. So, I take no chances. No, continue up. I know the steps be-

92

come uneven. Balance yourself against the wall.''

The steps were rough, unfinished, and several had no more than toe space.

''This was deliberate?'' asked Saraidh, beginning to show the effort of the climbing. ''Oh, for a grav shaft!''

Benden was in agreement as he felt the muscles in his calves and thighs tightening. And he had thought that he'd spent adequate time in p.t. to keep himself fit for any exertion.

''Now where?'' Saraidh asked as she came to a very narrow landing. The thin slit of a tiny aperture did nothing to illuminate the blank walls all around them.

Shensu apologized as he squeezed past the two officers, the half smile still on his face and, to their chagrin, he was showing no signs of effort. He put his hand, palm down, on a rough, apparently natural, declivity in the wall and suddenly a whole section of the wall pivoted inward. Light came on to illuminate a low deep cave. Benden whistled in surprise because the space was full of sacks, each tagged with some sort of coded label. Sacks of fuel, row upon row of them.

"There's more here than we need," Saraidh said, having made some rough calculations. "More than enough. But," and now she turned to Shensu, her expression stern, "I could understand your keeping this from Kimmer, but surely this was fuel those shuttles could have used? Or did they?" For she had also noticed that some of the closer ranks were thinner where sacks had obviously been removed.

Shensu held up his hand. "My father was an honorable man. And when the need arose, he took what was needed from this cavern and gave it, willingly, to Admiral Benden, doing all within his power to help overcome the menace that dropped from the skies. If he had not been murdered — "

Shensu broke off the sentence, his jaw muscles tensing, his expression bleak. "I do not know where the three shuttles went, but they could only have lifted from Landing on the fuel my father gave Admiral Benden. Now I give the rest of the fuel to a man also named Benden." Shensu looked pointedly at the lieutenant.

"Paul Benden was my uncle," he admitted, finding himself chagrined at this unexpected inheritance. "The *Erica* is also economical with fuel. With a full tank, we can lift you and even make some allowance for personal effects. But why is the fuel *here*?"

"My father did not steal it," Shensu said, indignant.

"And I didn't imply that he had, Shensu," Benden replied soothingly.

"My father accumulated this fuel during the transfer from the colony ships to the surface of the planet. He was the most accomplished shuttle pilot of them all. And he was the most economical. He only took what his careful flying saved on each flight and no one took harm from his economy. He told me how much was wasted by the other pilots, carelessly wasted. He was a charterer and had the right to take what was available. He merely ensured that fuel was available."

"But — " Benden began, wishing to reassure Shensu.

"He saved it to fly. He had to fly," and Shensu's eyes became slightly unfocused as his impassioned explanation continued. "It was his life. With space denied him, he designed a little atmosphere plane. I can show it to you. He flew it here, in Honshu, where no one but us could see him. But he took each of us up in that plane." Shensu's face softened with those memories. "That was the prize we all worked for. And I could understand his fascination with flight." Shensu took in a deep breath and regarded the two Fleet officers in his usual inscrutable fashion.

"I'm not sure I could live happily stuck landside forever," Benden said earnestly. "And we're grateful to be taken into your confidence, Shensu."

"My father would be pleased that his saving ways permit a Benden to save his

97

kinsmen,'' Shensu said in a wry tone
and with a sly glance at the lieutenant.
''But we will wait until late tonight,
when there are few to notice our activity.
Those marines of yours look strong. But
do not bring that ensign. He talks too
much. I do not want Kimmer to know of
our transaction. It is enough that he will
be rescued from Pern.''

''Have you checked these sacks recently, Shensu?'' Saraidh asked and,
when he shook his head, she had to
crouch to enter the low cave and inspect
the nearest. ''Your father did well,
Shensu,'' she said over her shoulder,
peering at the sack she had tilted upside
down. ''I was afraid there might be some
contamination from the plastic after
fifty-odd years but the fuel all seems to
be clear, no sediment, well saved.''

''What gemstones would be worth
bringing with us?'' Shensu asked casu-
ally.

''Industrial technology requires
quantities of sapphire, pure quartz, diamonds,'' Saraidh told him as she left the

cave, arching her back to relieve the strain of crouching. "But the major use of natural gemstones is once again decorative — for pets, high-status women, courtly men."

"Black diamonds?" Shensu asked, his lips parting in anticipation.

"Black diamonds!" Saraidh was astonished.

"Come, I will show you," Shensu said, allowing his lips to part in a pleased smile. "First we will close the cave and then descend to our workshops. Then I will show you the rest of the Hold as I said I would do," and he grinned back at them.

Benden was not sure whether going down was worse than climbing. He felt not only dizzy from the short arc of the stairs but had the sensation that he would fall forward down this interminable spiral. He considered himself competent in free fall or in space walking but this was a subtly different activity. He was only marginally relieved that Shensu was in front of him but, if

Saraidh fell into him, was Shensu sturdy
enough to keep all three from pitching
down?

They passed several landings, which
Shensu ignored, and seemed to descend
a very long way before they emerged
into another large room which must be
under the main living chamber. It was
not as high-ceilinged or as well finished,
but it was clearly furnished for a variety
of activities. He identified a large kiln, a
forge hearth, and three looms. Work
tables were placed near racks of carefully
stored tools. Hand tools, not a power
tool among them.

Shensu led them to plastic cabinets a
meter high and wide with many small
drawers. He pulled out two, evidently at
random, and scattered their contents on
the nearby table, the facets of the cut
stones sparkling in the overhead light.
Saraidh exclaimed in surprise, scooping
up a handful of carelessly thrown stones
of all sizes. Benden picked a large one
out of her hand, holding it up to the
light. He'd never seen anything like it,

dark but glittering with light.

"Black diamond. There's a whole beach full of them below a dead volcano," Shensu said, leaning back against the table, arms folded across his chest. His smile was amused. "We have drawers of them, along with emeralds, sapphires, rubies. We're all good lapidaries, though Faith is cleverest in cutting. We don't bother much with what Kimmer terms semi-precious stones, though he has some fine turquoise which he says is extremely valuable."

"Probably," Saraidh murmured, still absorbed in running a shower of the diamonds through her hands. She was absorbed but not, Benden noted, covetous.

"The blacks are why I know you won't find any survivors in the north," Shensu went on, his eyes on Benden who was less involved in the gemstones.

"Oh, why?"

"Before the sled power-packs died, Kimmer made two trips to Bitkim Island where he and Avril Bitra had mined both the black diamonds and emeralds. He

brought me and Jiro with him both times to help gather the rough diamonds. I saw him leave our camp late one night and I followed him. He went into a big water cavern before he disappeared from view. He had the light. I didn't dare go further. But, in the cavern lagoon three ships were moored, masts lashed to the decks. They were plastic hulled and their decks were badly scored by Thread. It couldn't pierce plastic but it could melt grooves on it. I went down into one of the ships and everything was neatly stowed aboard, even in the galley, where there were supplies in tight containers. Everything left in readiness for the ships to be sailed out of the cavern again.'' Shensu paused dramatically. Shensu had a feeling for the dramatic, Benden realized. But that was not a fault. "Three years later, we came back for a last load. And no one had been near the ships. There was a thick coat of dust on everything. Nothing had been touched. Except there was a lot more algae on the hulls and wind-blown debris on the

decks. Three years! I say there was no one left to sail them."

Saraidh had let the diamonds drip through her fingers to the table and now she sighed. "You said there was a volcanic island? Was it active when you were there? That could account for that heat source we noticed," she added to Benden.

"Kimmer would stretch the truth every which way," Shensu said, "to make himself look good. But he desperately wanted to have a larger gene pool — for his own pleasure if not ours." The last was said with an understandable malice. "If only a few more had survived, there'd be that much more future for all of us."

That gave both Ross Benden and Saraidh Ni Morgana a lot to mull over as Shensu showed them round the additional facilities: the animal barns, the well-supplied storage areas. He paused at a locked door to a lower level.

"Kimmer keeps the key to the hangar so I can't show you my father's plane,"

Shensu said. Then he gestured for them to ascend the stairs to the upper floors. Benden was relieved that these steps were wide and straight.

When they returned to the main level of Honshu Hold, they found the women busily preparing a feast; certainly a feast for those who had been five years on a mission. Not that the *Amherst* did not cater well but nothing to compare with spit-roasted lamb and the variety of Pernese hybrid vegetables and tubers. The two marines who stayed aboard, despite the slightly sarcastic assurance from Kimmer that no enemies could be lurking on Honshu Cliff, were brought heaping platters and non-fermented beverages by Faith and Charity. Within the Hold, the evening was merry and Kimmer, with a glass or two of wine, became expansive as a host. For he had recovered his composure after a long rest, and tactfully, no mention was made of his collapse.

As prearranged, Benden, Sergeant Greene, and Vartry met Shensu, his two brothers and the boys, Alun and Pat. Even with nine to tote sacks, it took four trips to top off the *Erica*'s tanks. The boys were short enough to walk upright in the low cave and they brought the sacks out to those who waited to haul them down. The marines were not above showing off their fitness and, using slings, carried eight sacks at a time. Ross Benden decided that four was quite enough and he had no reason to challenge the marines. The Fusaiyuki brothers carried six effortlessly. When the tanks were full, there were still sacks in the cavern.

THE NEXT MORNING, HEARING Nev's cheerful morning ablutions, Ross Benden stirred and abruptly stopped. He was uncomfortably stiff and sore from the night's exertions.

"Something wrong, sir?"

"Not a thing," Benden said. "Just finish up and let me have a chance, will you?"

Nev took that in good part and shortly was out of the tiny cabin. Moving with extreme caution, and hissing at the pain of abused muscles, Ross Benden managed to get to his feet. Bent-kneed, he hobbled to the hand-basin and opened the small cabinet above that contained the medical kit. A thorough search revealed nothing for muscular aches. He fumbled for a pain tablet, knocked it to the back of his mouth, and discovered that his neck was sore too. He took a drink of water. He must remember to drain the cistern and fill it with the excellent water of Pern.

A scratch at the door made Benden straighten up, despite the anguish to the long tendons in his legs, but he was damned if he'd show weakness.

"It's I," and Ni Morgana entered, taking in at a glance his semi-crippled state. "I thought this likely. Just one trip up and down those racks of a stair and my legs are sore. Faith gave me this salve — wanted me to test it to see if it was something of medical value. It's indigenous. No, lie back down, Ross, I'll slather it on. Supposed to have numbing properties. Hmm, it does," and she eyed her fingers and the generous dollop she had scooped out of the jar.

Ross was crippled enough to be willing to try anything, noxious or bizarre. He could hardly appear before Kimmer in his present shape.

"Oh, it is numbing. Whee, ooh, ahh, more on the right calf, please," Benden said, ridiculously relieved by the numbing effect of the salve. The pain seemed to drain out of his calves and thighs, leaving them oddly cool but not cold, and certainly free of that damnable soreness.

"I've got plenty for later and Faith says they have buckets of the stuff. Make it fresh every year. Doesn't smell half bad either. Pungent and — piney."

When she finished doctoring Benden, she washed her hands thoroughly. "I'd say don't shower today or you'll lose the relief." Then she turned back to Ross Bender, with a puzzled expression. "Ross," she began, settling against the little hand-basin and crossing her arms.

"How much would you say Kimmer weighed?"

"Hmm," and Benden thought of the man's build and height, "about 72-74 kilos. Why?"

"I weighed him in at 95 kilos. Of course, he was clothed, and the tunic and trousers are rather full and made of sturdy fabric, but I wouldn't have thought he carried that much flesh."

"Nor would I."

"I didn't judge the women correctly either. They all weighed in a little under or a little over 70 kilos and none of them are either tall or heavy-set."

Nev mumbled figures under his breath. "All of 'em, even the kids?"

"No, the three brothers are 73, 72, and 75 kilos which is about what I thought they'd be. The girl and the boys are also 2 or 3 kilos more than I'd have thought them."

"With a full tank, we can afford a few extra kilos," Benden said.

"I was also asked how much they could bring with them," Saraidh went on, "and I said we had to calibrate body weights and other factors before we could give them an exact allowance. I trust that wasn't out of line."

"I'll get Nev to calculate in those weights and let me know how much fuel we'll have in reserve then," Benden said. "And what we use as padding and safety harness so no one bounces all over the gig during take-off."

Folding out the cabin's keyboard, Benden ran some rough figures against the lifting power of the now full tank.

"D'you have a total on their weights?" Ni Morgana gave him the figure. He added them in plus kilos for padding and harness and contemplated the result. "I'd hate to be considered mean but 23.5 kilos each is about all we can allow."

"That's as much as we're allowed for personal effects on the *Amherst*," Ni Morgana said. "Is there room for 23.5 kilos in medicinals? I gather this stuff is effective."

"It certainly is," Benden said, flexing

110

his knees and feeling no discomfort.

"I'll just get some of this on the marines as well, then," Ni Morgana said.

"Ha!" was Benden's scoffing reply.

"I don't know about that," Ni Morgana said with a sly grin. "But then, you didn't catch sight of Sergeant Greene making for the galley. I think," and she paused reflectively, "that I'm doing some empirical tests of this junk and they just got lucky to be chosen as test subjects. Yes, that should save face admirably. We can't give Kimmer any reason to be suspicious, now, can we?" Then she left, chuckling over her subterfuge.

At 08:35, when Benden left the galley and proceeded to the Hold, he found Kimmer and the women in the main room, none of them looking too happy.

"We've done the calculations, Kimmer, and we can allow each of you, the children included, 23.5 kilos of personal effects. That's what Fleet personnel are generally allowed to bring on voyages

111

and I can't see Captain Fargoe objecting to it."

"Twenty-three point five kilos is quite generous, Lieutenant," Kimmer surprised Benden by saying. He turned to them chidingly. "That's more than we had coming out on the *Yoko*."

"And," Benden said, turning to Faith, "that wouldn't include medicinal products and respective seeds to a similar limit. Lieutenant Ni Morgana is of the opinion that they could well be valuable commodities."

"For which we'd be reimbursed?" asked Kimmer sharply.

"Of course," Benden said, keeping his voice even. "We have to allow for the weight of padding and harness to keep you secure during our drop into the primary's gravity well."

Charity and Hope emitted nervous squeaks.

"Nothing to worry yourself over, ladies," Benden went with a reassuring smile. "We use gravity wells all the time as a quick way to break out of a system."

"Be damned grateful we're getting off this frigging forsaken mudball," Kimmer said, angrily rising to his feet.

"Go on, now, sort out what you've got to bring but keep it to the weight limit. Hear me?"

The women removed themselves, with Faith casting one last despairing glance over her shoulder at her father. Benden wondered why he had thought any of them were graceful. They waddled in a most ungainly fashion.

"You've been extremely generous, Lieutenant," Kimmer said, affably as he settled himself again in the high-backed carved chair that he usually occupied at the table. "I thought we'd be lucky enough to get off with what we have on our backs."

"Are you absolutely positive that there are no other survivors on Pern?" Benden said, favoring a direct attack.

"Others could have carved holds out of cliffs and remained secure from that airborne menace of yours."

"Yes, they could have but, for one

thing, there aren't any cave systems here on the southern continent. And I'll tell you why I think the rest perished after I lost the last radio contact with those at Drake's Lake and Dorado. In those days I was more confident of rescue and I'd enough power left in my sled to make one more trip back to Bitkim Island where I'd mined some good emeralds." He paused, leaning forward, elbows on the table and shaking one finger at Benden. "And black diamonds."

"*Black* diamonds?" And Benden thought he sounded genuinely amazed.

"Black diamonds, a whole beach full of them. That's what I intend to bring back."

"Twenty-three point five kilos of them?"

"And a few pieces of turquoise that I also found."

"Really?"

"When I'd enough of a load of stones, I went into a natural cavern on Bitkim's southeast side. Big enough to anchor ships in if you stepped the mast.

And it was there.''

"Pardon?''

"Jim Tillek's ship was there, mast and all, holes and grooves where Thread had scored it time and again.''

"Jim Tillek?''

"The admiral's right hand. And a man who loved that ship. Loved it like other men love women — or Fussy Fusi loved flying,'' Kimmer allowed his malice to show briefly, "but I'm telling you, Jim Tillek wouldn't have left that ship, not to gather dust and algae on her hull if he was alive somewhere on Pern. And that ship had been anchored there three or four years. That's one very good reason why I know no one was left alive.

"Did you find any sign of human occupation,'' Kimmer went on, his voice less intense, his eyes glittering almost mockingly, "when you spiraled down across the northern hemisphere?''

"No, neither on infra or power-use detection,'' Benden had to admit.

Kimmer spread both arms wide then. "You know there's no one there, then.

115

No need to waste your reserves of fuel to find 'em. We're the last alive on Pern and, I'll tell you this, it's no planet for mankind."

"I'm sure the Colonial Authority will want a full report from you when we return to Base, Kimmer. I shall certainly log in my findings."

"Then do mankind a favor, Lieutenant, and tag this disaster of a world as uninhabitable!"

"That's not for me to say."

Kimmer snorted and sat back in his chair.

"Now, if you'll excuse me, I must join Lieutenant Ni Morgana on her scientific survey. There are sufficient lift-belts, if you'd like to come along."

"No, thank you, Lieutenant," and Kimmer flicked his hand in dismissal of such activity. "I've seen about as much of this planet as I have any wish to."

BENDEN WAS JUST STRAPPING ON his lift belt when Kimmer erupted from the Hold, the whites of his eyes showing in his agitation.

"Lieutenant!" he cried, running towards the small party.

Benden held up a warning hand as one of the marines beside him moved to intercept the man.

"Lieutenant, what power do you use for the belts? What power?" Kimmer cried excitedly as he approached.

"Pack power, of course," Benden replied.

"Regulation packs?" And, without apology, Kimmer grabbed the lieutenant by the shoulder and swung him round, just as Vartry took hold of the old man's arm.

"As you were!" Ross Benden barked at the marine but with a nod to reassure him, because he understood what Kimmer, in his excitement, did not explain. "Yes, standard power-packs and we have enough to reactivate that sled of yours, if it's in any reasonable working order."

"It is, Lieutenant, it is!" Kimmer reassured him, his agitation replaced by immense satisfaction. "So you'll be able to eyeball the remains of the colony and report honestly to your captain that you followed your orders, Mister Benden," and Kimmer stressed the name in a tone just short of malice, "as assiduously as your noble relative would have done." Ross grimaced, but his relation to the admiral would have become public sooner or later. "I thought you looked familiar," Kimmer added, smugly.

Benden took the lieutenant aside for a quick conference and she concurred that it was Benden's first obligation to search as far as he was able for survivors. She was quite willing to conduct her own scientific research with Shensu as her guide and two marines as assistants. So she wished the lieutenant good luck and lifted gracefully off the plateau, floating down in the direction of the nearest evidence of Thread, some ten klicks down the valley on the other side of the river.

That matter settled, Kimmer began to pluck at Benden's sleeve in his urgency and hurried him, Nev following, back into the Hold. Maps were still spread out on the table from the previous evening.

"I searched east as far as Landing and Cardiff," Kimmer said, prodding one map with an arthritic index finger. He dragged it back and down along to the Jordan River. "Those Stakes were all empty and Thread-ridden though Calusa, Ted Tubberman's old place wasn't." Kimmer frowned a moment, then shrugged off that enigma, moving his finger up to the coastline and west. "Paradise River must have been used as some kind of staging area because there were netted containers in the overgrowth along the shore, but the buildings were all boarded up. Malay, too, and Boca," he stabbed again at those points on the map. "I went north from Boca to Bitkim, but I confess that I didn't stop at Thessaly or Roma where they had well-built stone houses and barns. And I didn't get any further west. The gauge on the power-pack was jiggling too much for me to risk getting stranded.''

''So there could be survivors to the west . . .'' Benden pored over the map, feeling a surge of excitement and hope. Then he wondered why Kimmer was willing to take such a risk — that enough survivors would be found for the colony to be left to work out its parochial problems. Maybe the prospect of leaving so much behind, including being the default owner of a planet, was giving Kimmer second thoughts. If fifty years of his life's endeavors was going to be crammed into a 23.5 kilo sack. living out the remainder of his life in the comforts he had achieved might indeed hold more charm for the old man than an uncertain, and possibly, pauper's existence in a linear warren.

''There could indeed be Stakeholders there, but why haven't they attempted any contact?'' Kimmer asked defiantly and his eyes quickly concealed a flicker of something else. ''I got the last communication from the west but that could have been for any number of reasons.

"Now, if you've got a portable unit that we could bring with us, maybe closer to one of the western Stakes, we might rouse someone."

"Let's see this sled of yours." Benden didn't mention that they had opened the broadest range of communications on their inbound spiral with not so much as a flicker on any frequency. But Kimmer was right that lack of communication could have been caused by any number of reasons.

Kimmer led them to the locked door which he opened and proceeded down to the next level, a hangar in fact, with wide double doors at one end which opened out on the wide terrace below the Hold entrance plateau. While the sled occupied the center of the considerable floor space, Kenjo's little atmosphere underwing craft, was not quite hidden in the back. Then Benden's attention was all for the sled which was cocooned in the usual durable thin plastic film. This Kimmer energetically punc-

tured. All four men helped peel the sled free as Kimmer enumerated his exact shut-down precautions. Although the plas canopy was somewhat darkened with age and the tracks of Thread hits, when Benden touched the release button, the door slid back as easily as if it had been opened the day before.

This was a much older model than those now in use, of course, so Benden did a thorough inspection. The fabric of the sturdy vessel was undamaged. The control panel was one he recognized from text-tapes. When he depressed the power toggle, the gauge above it fluttered and then dropped back to zero. He walked aft to the power locker, flipped up the latches on the power trunk, and lifted the big unit out to examine the leads. Liftbelts used much smaller packs, but Benden could see no difficulty in making a multiple connection of smaller units to supply power. Moving forward again, Kimmer stepping out of his way but exuding a palpable excitement, Benden tested the steering yoke

123

which moved easily in his grip.

"We'll just make a link-up and see how she answers to power. Ensign Nev, take Kimo and Jiro and break out twelve belt packs, and the portable com-unit. We're going to take a little ride."

An hour later, once more operational, the old sled drifted under its own power to the narrow lower terrace.

When Benden returned to the *Erica* for rations and a bedroll, an earnest and anxious Nev accosted him, wanting to join the expedition.

"You don't know what that old man might try, Lieutenant. And I don't trust him."

"Listen up," Benden said in a low and forceful tone that stopped Nev's babbling. "I'm not half as worried about my safety as I am about the *Erica*'s. Kimmer goes with me. I don't trust him either. I'll take Jiro along as well. And Sergeant Greene. Neither of them could get through Greene to me. You'll only have Kimo to worry about and he strikes me as too placid to do anything on his own. Shensu is a proven ally. Present my compliments to Lieutenant Ni Morgana when she returns and relay this order. Either you or the lieutenant are to be on the *Erica* at all times. The marines are to stand proper watches until I return. Have I made that clear?"

"Aye, aye, sir, Lieutenant Benden. Loud and clear, sir." Nev's teeth were almost chattering with his assurances and his eyes were wide as he dutifully assimilated his orders.

"I'll report in at intervals so break out hand-units for yourself and Vartry."

"Aye, aye, sir."

"We'll be back in two days." He ordered Greene to collect supplies and carry them to the sled.

"If you will pardon me, Lieutenant," Kimmer said unctuously as he and Jiro entered the craft, "I think we can easily reach Karachi Camp today, stopping at Suweto and Yukon on the way. Karachi is a real possibility because, now that Thread is gone, they'd want to activate the mines."

125

Surprising himself, Benden gestured with an open hand to the pilot's seat. "You have the con, Mr. Kimmer." It was as good a way as any to see just how competent the old man had been, if he had actually done what he'd said he'd done. "After all, you're more familiar with this model sled than I am and you know where we're going." It would also be easier to keep the old man occupied.

So Benden seated himself behind Kimmer while the sergeant, giving the officer only a mildly reproachful look, took the seat next to Jiro on the starboard side.

The old sled purred along as if delighted by its release from long imprisonment. It answered the yoke with the smoothness of a well-maintained vehicle as Kimmer swung it to port. Kimmer wasn't all bad, Benden thought to himself, and wondered again why the old man had insisted on this search. Was it really to prove to Benden that his folk were the only ones left? Or had Kimmer some ulterior motive? And would Kim-

126

mer be surprised if they did find anyone? After overflying the snowy waste
of the northern continent and the devastation of the southern lands, Benden
could only be surprised that anyone had
survived. It was certainly most unlikely
that his uncle, who'd be well into his
twelfth decade, would still be alive.

They came down from the foothills
across the river, obliquely to port of Ni
Morgana and her group, and then across
a lifeless plain of circles in the dust.
There were spots here and there of
struggling plant life but Benden wondered if the wind would scatter the top
soil before vegetation could reestablish
itself and prevent further erosion. And
that was the pattern for the next few
hours — broad uneven-edged ribbons,
about fifty klicks across of ravaged land
— then broader belts of grassland or
forest, even thick vegetation neither
shrub or jungle, with the glint of hidden
water in rivers and ponds.

The old sled purred along at about
220 klicks per hour. Benden broke out

rations and passed them around. Kimmer altered the course and, over the sloping nose of the sled, a large and brilliantly blue lake could be seen. As they neared it and Kimmer obligingly skimmed low, vegetation crowned mounds indicated the ruins of a considerable settlement.

"Drake's Lake," and Kimmer gave a sour laugh. "Damned arrogant fool," he muttered to himself. "No signs of anyone but there may be at Andiyar's mines."

They overflew more deserted housing and startled a herd of grazing animals who plunged wildly away from the muted sound of the sled.

"Livestock seems to have survived," Benden remarked. "Will you turn yours loose?"

"What else?" and Kimmer barked a laugh. "Though Chio's moaning about her pet fire-dragon having to be left behind."

"Fire-dragon?" Benden asked in surprise.

128

"Well, that's what some people thought they looked like," Kimmer explained diffidently. "They look like reptiles, lizards to me. It's an indigenous life-form, hatches from eggs, and if you get one then, it attaches itself to you. Useless thing as far as I can see but Chio's fond of it." He glanced over his shoulder at Benden.

"It wouldn't take up much room," Jiro said, speaking for the first time. "It's a bronze male."

Benden shook his head. "Humans, yes, creatures no," he said firmly. The captain was still likely to question his foisting eleven human survivors on her but she'd blow her tubes if he tried to impose an alien pet.

They reached the mine site and landed near the adits. Within was cocooned equipment — ore carts, picks, shovels, all kinds of hand tools, as well as an array of tough plas props for tunnel supports.

"You really had gone back to the lowest level of useful technology, hadn't

129

you?" Benden said, hefting on the picks. "But if you had stone cutters, didn't you — "

"When that damned Thread started falling, your uncle called in all power-packs for use in the sleds. That was Benden's priority and we couldn't fight it."

The living quarters, unlike those at the lake, had been cocooned. Peering in through the thinner patches over windows, Benden could see that furnishings had been left in place.

"See what I mean, Lieutenant. This place is all ready to be started up again. It's nearly two years since Thread stopped falling. If they could, they'd be back here."

They spent the night there at Kara-chi, setting up a rough camp. While Kimmer started a fire, 'to keep the tunnel snakes away' he told Benden, the lieutenant made contact with Honshu and spoke to Nev who said the lieutenant was writing up her notes and that nothing of any significance had happened.

Just as Benden was signing off, Jiro came to the sled for a coil of rope and walked off into the forest. He returned not too much later with a fat squat avian which he had roped off a branch and strangled. He identified it as a wherry, as he neatly skinned and spitted it over the fire. During its roasting, the aroma of the meat was tantalizing, arousing a good appetite. It proved to be very tasty.

"Forest wherries are better than coastal ones," Kimmer said, slicing himself another portion. "Those have an oily, fishy taste."

Greene nodded appreciatively as he licked his fingers clean of the juices. Then he excused himself and disappeared into the woods. Just about the time Benden was becoming apprehensive about his long absence, he reappeared.

"Nothing moving anywhere, except things that slither," he reported to the lieutenant in a low voice. "I don't think we need to set a watch, Lieutenant, but

I always sleep light."

As Benden saw Kimmer already asleep and Jiro settling down on their side of the fire, he decided a watch would be superfluous tonight. The enemies of this deserted world had retreated into space.

"I sleep light, too, Greene." And he did, rousing often during the night at slight unaccustomed sounds, Kimmer's intermittent snores, or when Jiro added more wood to the fire.

In the morning, Benden contacted Honshu and this time spoke with Ni Morgana who said that her expedition had been entirely successful — from the scientific point of view. She would spend the day cataloguing the medicinal plants and their properties with the women. Benden gave her the day's flight plan and signed off.

They doubled back east and slightly north of the mining site and Drake's Lake, then followed a fairly wide river as it flowed down to the distant sea. And came upon the stout stone houses and barns that had housed the inhabitants of Thessaly and Roma. They observed herds of beasts, cattle, and sheep in nearby fields but the houses, and barns, had been cleared of all effects. Now just dead leaves and other debris littered the spacious rooms where the shutters had fallen from rusted hinges.

"Lieutenant," and Greene motioned for him to step a little away from the other two men, "we haven't seen any of the sleds Kimmer said they used. Nor those three missing shuttles. So, if we find them, wouldn't we find the people?"

"We would, if we could, Sergeant," Benden said tiredly. "Kimmer, how long did your sled have power?"

Kimmer's eyes gleamed as he appreciated what Benden did not ask. "Once I reached Honshu, I didn't use the sled at all, except as a power source for the com-unit, for maybe five-six years. Ito got very sick and I went to Landing to see if I could get a medic out here. They'd all left and taken everything with them. I tried some other Stakes, as I told you, but they were deserted too. Ito died and I was too busy with the kids and then Chio to go off. Then I made one trip to Bitkim and four years later, as I'd no way to recharge the pack, I made that last trip. But," and he held up his gnarled finger, "like I told you, just before I lost all contact, I heard part of Benden's message to conserve all power. So they couldn't have had many operational sleds. I think," and here Kimmer paused to search his memory. His eyes met the lieutenant's. "I think they didn't have enough power left to go after Thread anymore and they were going to have to wait." He sighed. "That'd be forty years they'd've had to wait for the end of Thread, Lieutenant, and I don't think they made it."

"Yes, but where were they?"

Kimmer shrugged. "Hell, Lieutenant, if I knew that I'd've hiked across the continent to find them once Thread stopped. If I'd had one whisper, I'd've tracked it down." He swiveled about then, facing west. "They were some-place in the west from the direction of their signals. Say," and his face lit up suddenly, "maybe they went to Ierne Island. That would have been easier to protect than one of these open Stakes."

So Benden called in the new desti-nation. "We'll be back by tomorrow evening . . ."

"You'd better be," Ni Morgana said dryly. "That window won't wait for any-one."

There was no question in Benden's mind that the lieutenant would delay taking that window either but he wasn't worried about that. He had to be sure — and it looked as if Kimmer's conscience required him also to be confident that there was no one else alive of Benden's group.

The run to Ierne Island took most of the rest of that day and was as fruitless as the other. Kimmer suggested one fur-ther detour, to the tip of Dorado prov-ince, to Seminole and Key Largo Stakes. On the wreckage of a storm-damaged building, they found a com-mast, or sections of it, and evidence of a hurried departure of the inhabitants. In another shed, still partly roofed, the remains of two sleds were discovered, obviously broken up to provide spare parts. The canopies and hulls were well scored and blistered by Thread. Benden appreciated that Kimmer was extraordinarily lucky to have survived at all.

They made their evening camp there with Jiro providing fish which he caught from the remains of a sturdy jetty. The last ten meters, projecting out into the channel, had been snapped off by some tremendous storm, or maybe many. It took a lot of force to break off heavy duty plastic pilings like that.

When Ross Benden checked in with the *Erica*, he roused a sleepy Nev, forgetting that there was a time difference across the southern continent.

"Everything's okay," Nev said, interrupting himself with a yawn, "though the lieutenant is sure something's up. She says the women are acting funny."

136

"They're about to leave all they've known as well as a very comfortable life," Benden replied.

"Isn't that. Lieutenant'll tell you when you get back." Nev didn't seem much concerned but Benden trusted the lieutenant's instincts.

He was wakeful that night, trying to figure out what could have gone wrong. Kimmer was with him. Shensu was eager to leave, too. And with five to guard the *Erica*, which was Benden's main concern, what could go wrong?

He worried about that all the way back to Honshu which was a useless activity. But he'd noticed that those who anticipated problems always seemed able to solve them faster.

When they finally reached Honshu, despite the gathering dusk, Kimmer insisted on maneuvering the sled into its garage, proving his piloting skills.

"This sled's done more than its designers ever expected, Benden," Kimmer said sardonically as he reversed it in, "so humor an old man in rewarding its service the only way he can."

Benden and Greene left him and Jiro
to a ritualistic deservicing. Benden ran
up the stairs to the main room. Ni Morgana was there, storing small packages
in a case. Benden noticed first that some
of the wall hangings were missing and
then that the big room appeared to be
stripped. Damn it! They only had 23.5
kilos each.

"Glad to have you back, Ross," Ni
Morgana said, smiling a welcome.
"We're just about packed up and ready
to go." There was nothing in her manner
to suggest anxiety. "There you are,
Charity. If you'll stow that in the galley
locker, that's the last." She consulted her
notepad then, reading the last entry as
Charity left with the container. "From
your less than jubilant manner, Lieutenant, I gather that your time was wasted."

"You could gather that, Saraidh,"
Benden said, trying not to sound trucu-
lent. "In some places material was neatly
stored as if the owners intended to return; in others, everything had been left

open to the weather, or showed signs of hurried departure. They turned their animals loose and those have multiplied so I'd say that the meek have inherited this planet. You said you'd had more success?"

She reviewed her notepad a moment longer, then flipped it shut and placed it in a hip pocket. A nod of her head and both officers moved toward the door. Benden was relieved to see one of the marines on duty at the ramp of the *Erica*, having a word with Charity before she entered.

"When I've written up my investigations," she said with considerable satisfaction, "there're going to be some red faces. Irrefutably, the Oort cloud supports a life form which I have observed in its normal immensely sluggish metabolic, activated, and defunct states. Fascinating actually, even if it also has managed to devastate a world and ruin it for further human habitation." Ni Morgana walked Benden to the far side of the *Erica*, raising her arm as if to point

139

something out to him. "I don't know what's going on but something is, Ross. I don't believe it's just sorrow for leaving their home that's making the women nervous, jumpy, and accounts for a mass insomnia. The children seem fine and Shensu and Kimo have been most helpful."

"I thought taking Kimmer and Jiro with me was a sensible precaution."

"Sensible but Kimmer's quite likely to have given those women orders before he left. I think he did. I just don't know what. We haven't left the *Erica* unattended but each of us who's stood a watch on her has been plagued with headaches. I'll admit to you, Ross, that I fell asleep on watch. I can't have dozed for more than ten or twenty minutes but I was asleep. I can't get Cahill Nev or the other marines to admit that they had similar lapses but Nev had that hangdog expression I've come to know well in erring ensigns. Anyway, after my little snooze, Nev and I searched the ship from prow to the propulsion units and couldn't find anything illegally stowed. Which is what I think's been happening. Oh, we've put aboard everyone's 23.5 kilos, which were thoroughly searched and weighed before I'd permit them to stow it. Nothing hidden in anyone's bundle.

"And the women . . ." Ni Morgana paused, deep in thought and then shook her head slowly. "They're exhausted although they swear blind that they're fine, just that this has all happened so fast. Chio released that little dragoney pet of hers and she bursts into tears if you glance sidewise at her." Then she gave a chuckle. "Nev and I thought to cheer them up and he's a mainframe of humorous anecdotes about life in high tech. He's from a colonial family so he's been marvelous at reassuring them. You should have heard the spiel he gave on how they'll be living back on a 'civilized' planet and all the advantages of same. They cheered up a bit and then fall into the weeps again.

Then she turned briskly professional. "We've got additional safety harnesses for all, by the way, and pallets with a local vegetable sponge that is lightweight but cushioning. I figure that all the women should be strapped into the marines' bunks: the kids and the brothers can use the pallets and temporary harness in the wardroom and the marines will take the extra seats in the cabin with us. Tight squeeze but there're only so many places you can put bodies on this gig. Where is Kimmer?" she asked. "I think one of us ought to keep a close eye on his movements this evening." Then she looked out to the last of the brilliantly red and orange sunset. "Too bad. This is such a beautiful planet."

That night a lavish feast was spread for everyone — except the man on duty on the *Erica*. Kimmer urged the officers and the three marines to drink as much of his fine wines as possible for the tunnel snakes wouldn't appreciate them. When he found the Fleet reluctant to overindulge, he nagged the girls and

142

the three men to 'eat, drink, and be merry.' Taking his own advice, he passed out before the meal was finished.

"He'll have to be sober by . . ." and Benden consulted his digital to check, "09:00 tomorrow or he'll be nauseous in take-off and I don't want to have to clean that up when we reach free-fall. Good evening and thank you, Chio, for such a magnificent meal," he added and after Saraidh had also complimented the women, the *Erica*'s complement left.

Kimmer looked none the worse for the drink the next morning as he and the others reported on time to board the *Erica*. Nev strapped the Pernese in but Benden made a final check himself. The women were all red-eyed and Chio patently so nervous that he wondered if he should get Ni Morgana to give her a mild sedative.

At the exact second calculated by Lieutenant Zane, the *Erica* lifted from the plateau, blasting her way skyward, tail rockets blazing.

A FISHERMAN, STANDING THE DOG watch on his trawler off the coast of Fort Hold, saw the fiery trail, vivid against the gray eastern sky, and wondered at it. He followed the blazing lance of light until it was no longer visible. He wondered what it was but his more immediate concern was keeping warm and wondering if the cook had made klah by now and could he get a cup.

"THE ROLL RATE'S TOO LOW!" BENden cried over the roar of the engines, exerting all his strength to keep the right attitude. "She's a slug," and suddenly Benden realized that the *Erica*'s reluctance could be caused by only one thing. "We've got too much weight on board. She's too bloody heavy through the yoke," he said through gritted teeth. He forced his head to look to his right at Nev, strapped in the co-pilot's seat. Ni Morgana was in the next row with Greene beside her while the other marines stoically endured acceleration g-forces in makeshift couches. "I've got to

144

increase thrust. And that's going to take one helluva lot of fuel."

Benden made the adjustments, swearing bitterly to himself over the expenditure of so much fuel. His calculations could *not* be wrong. They were also too far gone in their path to abort and, if they did, there was no way to contact the *Amherst* and arrange a new rendezvous. How in hell could she be so heavy?

"Nev, give me some figures on what this is costing us in fuel and the estimated weight we're lugging up."

"Aye, aye, sir," Nev said, slowly moving his hand in the g-force to activate the armrest pad.

Benden forced his head to the side so he could see the bright green numbers leap to the small screen.

"Twenty-one minutes five seconds of blast, sir, was what we should have needed," Nev replied, his voice genuinely strained. "We're bloody twenty-nine point twenty into flight and still not free! We're — uh — four nine five point five six kilograms overweight! Free fall in ten seconds!"

Ten seconds seemed half a year until they were suddenly weightless. Benden swore as he read the ominous position of the fuel gauge. Still cursing, he adjusted her yaw with a burst of the port jets, swinging her nose towards the sun. He already knew that they hadn't enough fuel to make their scheduled rendezvous with the *Amherst*. And the cruiser would currently be in a communication's shadow as it made its parabolic turn about Rukbat.

He called up Rukbat's system on the console monitor. There was no way they could use the second planet as a slingshot. But, and he pulled at his lower lip, there was a chance they could make it to the first little burnt out cinder of a planet. They'd come awful close to Rukbat and even closer to the surface of Number One in order to use its gravity well. That would save fuel. But they'd need a different rendezvous point. That is, *if* they could get to the same point at the same time, at the same speed and heading in the same direction as the cruiser at some point earlier in her outbound hyperbolic orbit of Rukbat.

"Nev, figure me a slingshot course around the first planet." There was only the one option left to Benden.

"Aye, aye, sir," and the ensign's voice was full of relief.

Then in a taut hard voice, he shot out a second order. "Greene, bring me Kimmer. Tell the others to stay put."

He flipped open the harness release and let himself drift up out of the pilot's seat, trying to figure out just how Kimmer had managed to sneak 495.56 kilograms of whatever it was on board his ship. And when? Especially as the man had been under his watchful eye for over three days.

"Lieutenant," and Nev's voice was apologetic, "we can't make a slingshot around the first planet, not with the weight on board."

"Oh, we'll be lighter very soon, Nev," Benden replied with a malicious grin. "Four hundred ninety-five point fifty-six kilograms lighter. Figure a course with that weight loss."

"What I can't understand," Ni Morgana said in a flat voice, "is what they could have smuggled aboard. Or how?"

"What about your headaches, Saraidh?" Benden asked, seething with anger at Kimmer's duplicity. "And those catnaps no one else's had the guts to report to me."

"What could they possibly have done in ten or twenty minutes, Ross?" Ni Morgana demanded flatly, her nostrils flaring at his implication of dereliction of duty. "Nev and I searched for any possibly smuggled goods or tampering."

Benden said nothing, pointedly, and then scrubbed at his in frustration. "Oh, it's no blame to you, Saraidh. Kimmer just outsmarted me, that's all. I thought removing him from Honshu would solve the problem." He raised his voice. "Vartry, you, Scag, and Hemlet will conduct a search of the most unlikely places on this ship: the missile

bins, the head, the inner hull, the airlock. Somehow they've overloaded us
and we have got to know with what and
dump it!" He turned to Nev. "Try reaching the *Amherst*. I think it's too soon
to make contact but get on the blower
anyhow."

Kimmer overhanded himself into the
cabin then, a smile on his face for the
fierce expressions on the three marines
as they passed him by.

"Kimmer, what did you get on board
this ship and where is it, because we've
got less than an hour to make a course
correction, and thanks to you we've lost
too much fuel lifting the bird off Pern."

"I don't know what you mean, Lieutenant," was the reply and Kimmer
looked him squarely in the eye. "I was
with you for three days. How could I
have put something on board this vessel?"

"Stop stalling, man, it's your life
you'll lose as well."

"I'm flattered that you've asked my
opinion, Lieutenant, but I'm sure you
know better than I what equipment can

be jettisoned to lighten her."

Benden stared him down, wondering at the malevolence in the gaze Kimmer returned. "You know what weight I'm referring to and it was all put on at Honshu. If I don't know what that was, Kimmer, you'll be the first thing that lightens this gig's load."

Suddenly they all heard hysterical weeping from the stern and Vartry propelled himself back into the cabin.

"Lieutenant, they started the minute I said we were going to search because the ship was overweight. They know something!"

Benden hand-pushed himself deftly down the short companionway to the marines' quarters, the wailing rising to an eerie ululation that made the hairs on the back of his neck rise.

"Stow it!" Benden roared but Chio's volume only increased. The others were not as loud but just as distraught, plainly terrified and far too hysterical to reply to his demands for an explanation.

Ni Morgana arrived with the medical

kit and injected Chio with a sedative which reduced the hysterics but had no effect when Benden questioned her, trying to keep his voice level and reasonable.

"They will not tell you what they have done," Shensu said, careering into the marines' quarters. Absently rubbing the arm he had bruised, he looked down at Chio. "She has always been dominated by him and so have the others. If Kimmer can be made," and Shensu's voice was hard-edged with hatred, "to give them the necessary orders."

"I think Kimmer will explain, or take a long step out of a short airlock," Benden said, pushing past Shensu. There was no time for finesse or bluff with the *Erica* currently on an abortive course for the second planet. They had to make a correction soon. And do it without the excess weight or they'd be beyond rescue. He'd have the truth if he had to space Kimmer and enough of the women to get one of them to tell him what he had to know.

"Lieutenant!" Greene's booming voice was urgent and Benden propelled himself as fast as he could back to the cabin where Greene was searching Kimmer roughly. "Sir, he's wearing metal. I felt it when I frisked him." And as the sergeant peeled back the shipsuit, a vest was exposed, a vest made up of panels of gold. "Shit!"

"Hardly!" Kimmer remarked, smiling smugly.

"Strip him!" Benden ordered and not only was Kimmer wearing a gold vest but a thick belt of gold cast in lozenge shapes. His underpants had pockets filled with thin gold sheets. Greene was nothing if not thorough and even the boots on Kimmer's feet produced smaller gold plates worked into the soles and ankle leather.

"Saraidh!" Benden roared. "Search those women. Greene, you search the kids, but gently, get me? Shensu, Jiro, Kimo, in here on the double." Benden took some comfort when the three men proved to be wearing no more than their

153

shipsuits. Ni Morgana's yell confirmed Benden's guess about the women. All the while Kimmer kept in place his slight, amused smile. It took both Vartry and Saraidh to bring the concealed sheets and gold plates the women had secreted to the cabin.

"I'd estimate that's about ten to fifteen kilos per woman and five per kid," she said as they looked down at the pile of gold.

Benden shook his head. "Forty-five kilos is a drop! No where near four hundred ninety-five point fifty-six k's." He turned on the naked Kimmer who smiled back, all innocence. "Kimmer, we're running out of time. Now where is the rest of it? Or had you intended becoming an integral part of Rukbat?"

"You don't panic me, Lieutenant Benden," and Kimmer's eyes glittered with a vengeance that shocked Ross. "This ship's in no danger. Your cruiser'll rescue you."

Benden stared at the man in utter amazement. "The cruiser is behind Ruk-

bat, in com shadow. We can't arrange a
different rendezvous. Unless we can
lighten this ship, we can't even make a
course change for the one chance we
have of staying alive!" Benden hauled
Kimmer by the arm to the console and
showed him the diagram on the screen,
and the little blip that was the *Erica*,
serenely heading for her original, now
non-viable destination. "We certainly
don't have enough fuel to make the
arranged rendezvous." He tapped out
the sequence to show the original flight
plan. Then, with his finger, Benden indicated the inexorable path the *Erica* was
taking. "Tell us what and where the
excess weight is hidden, Kimmer!"

Kimmer contented himself with a
wry chuckle and Benden wanted to
smash it off his face. But Kimmer was
enjoying this too much to give him that
satisfaction.

"If that's the way you want to play
it, Kimmer. Sergeant, get the stuff and
bring it with you," and Benden hustled
the naked barefooted colonist down the

companionway to the airlock and, palm-
ing the control for the inner hatch,
shoved Kimmer inside, motioned for
Greene to throw in the gold, and closed
the hatch again.

"I mean it, Kimmer, either tell me
what else is on board and where, or you
go out the airlock."

Kimmer turned, a contemptuous expression on his face, and he folded his
arms across his chest, a gaunt old man
with only defiance to clothe him.

"You've more than enough fuel, Benden. Chio checked the gauge. The *Erica*'s
tanks were full. Since you had to have
used at least a third of a tank to get here,
I'm of the opinion that Shensu knew,"
and his eyes traveled to Benden's left
where Shensu was standing by the window, "as I always suspected, where
Kenjo had stored his pilferings." Kimmer drew himself up. "No, Lieutenant,
I will call your bluff."

"It's no bluff, Kimmer, and if you
had any training as a space jockey,
you'd've felt how sluggish the gig was.

156

She's heavy, too heavy. We burned too much in the lift-off. The gold on you and the women isn't enough to cause that. Dammit, Kimmer, it's your life, too."

"I'll have taken a Benden down with me," the man said in a snarl of hatred and sheer malevolence, his face contorted.

"But Chio, and your daughters, your grandchildren — " Benden began.

"They were none of them worth the effort I put into them," Kimmer replied arrogantly. "I have to share my wealth with them but I'm certainly not sharing it with you."

"Sharing?" Benden stared at him, not quite comprehending the man's words. "You think I'm blackmailing you? For a share of your wealth?" The disgust in Benden's voice momentarily rattled the man. "There are many people in *my* world, Kimmer, who are not motivated by greed." He gestured with contemptuous anger at the sheets and lozenges at Kimmer's feet. "None of that is worth the risk you want us to take. What have you hidden on the *Erica* and where?"

Just then, Ni Morgana beckoned urgently to Benden. He gratefully moved away from the window. His hand hovered briefly over the evac button. Kimmer could stay where he was, just a thin sheet away from space, and contemplate his situation.

"When I was looking for tranqs, I came across a vial of scopalamine in the medical chest. It may be an anesthetic, but the right dosage also provides the truth — so Chio spilled it out. It's platinum and germanium, sheets of it, stuffed wherever they could when they came aboard on legitimate errands," she said, her voice low enough for Benden's ears only, "and when they drugged whoever was on the dogwatch. That's why we all had headaches."

"Platinum? Germanium?" Benden was astounded.

"Kimmer was a mining engineer. He found ores and we've all had to work in them," Shensu said, pushing over to them. "I wondered why the workroom smelled of hot metal. He must have had the girls melt the ingots down at night, extruding sheets. No wonder they've looked so worn out. I never thought to check on the metals because they'd be too heavy to bring."

"Where is it?" Benden demanded, looking up and down the aisle, momentarily bewildered when he thought of all the places sheets of thin metal could be unobtrusively attached within the *Erica*. "We've got to search the ship! Everywhere! Sergeant, take your marines to the stern. Shensu, you and your brothers start on the lockers."

"He knew one helluva lot about the interior of gigs," Nev remarked almost admiringly when the marines found that the missile tubes had been stuffed with metal plaques. These were immediately flushed into space.

"And I watched her, Lieutenant," Vartry said, aggrieved, when they found that the locker where the medicines had been stowed was also lined with thin slabs of silvery metal. "I stood here and

159

watched her, heard her tell me she wanted to be sure the medicines were safe, as she slapped sheets top, bottom, and side."

The lockers in which the 23.5 kilo personal allowances had been stowed also proved to be lined with platinum.

"You know," Ni Morgana said, bending one of the thin sheets which she had found under Benden's bunk, "individually these don't weigh much but they damned near coated the gig with 'em. Ingenious."

There were sheets everywhere and still more was found, to be piled at the airlock hatch.

Nev, remembering how he'd entertained Hope and Charity by showing them the cabin, found metal glued to the bottom of the blast couches, lining the inside of the control panel, and thin rolls of metal tacked to the baseboards, looking for all the worlds like innocuous decorations. The viewports had platinum decorated seals. That sent Nev and Scag searching all the ports.

When the pile at the inner airlock door reached the window, abruptly Benden realized the airlock was empty.

"Kimmer? Where's Kimmer?" he cried. Who let him out? Where is he?"

But Kimmer was nowhere in the ship. A gesture from Benden had the marines on his heels as they propelled themselves to the galley where the brothers were still searching.

"Which of you depressed the evac button?" Benden demanded, seething with impotent anger.

"Depressed . . ." Shensu's look of astonishment was, Benden felt, genuine. There was no regret, however, on his face or his brothers'.

"I'm not sure I blame you, Shensu, but it constitutes murder. You had opportunities enough while we were searching the ship."

"We were searching the ship, too," Shensu said with dignity. "We were as busy as you, trying to save our lives."

"Perhaps," Jiro said softly, "he committed suicide rather than face the failure

161

of that brainstorm of his."

"That is a possibility," Ni Morgana said, composedly but Benden knew she believed that no more than he did. But it was true that, although Kimmer could not have activated the inner hatch of the airlock, the evac button on the outer door was clearly marked. And the mechanism cycled itself shut in two minutes after use.

"This will be investigated more fully when we have time," Ross Benden promised them fervently, pinning each of the three brothers with his angry glare. "I won't condone murder!" Though at just that moment, Benden had several he would like to commit.

Returning to the airlock, he found that Nev was busy with a chisel, letting out a hoot of triumph as he peeled off a paper thin sheet of platinum.

"I'm sure Captain Fargoe wouldn't mind having a platinum plated gig . . ." His voice trailed off when he caught sight of Benden's expression. He gulped. "There'd be another twenty ki-

162

los right in here." And he applied himself to the task of removing it.

Benden signaled for two of the marines to assist Nev while he and the others piled the accumulated sheets, pipings, strips and lozenges into the lock.

"Amazing!" Ni Morgana said, shaking her head wearily. "That ought to make up the rest of the 495.56 kilos."

She stepped out of the lock and gestured to Benden who was at the controls. With a feeling of intense relief, he pressed the evac button and saw the metal slid slowly out into space, a glittering cascade left behind the *Erica*. It was still visible as the outer door cycled shut.

"I've half a mind to add their personal allowances," Benden began, feeling more vicious and vengeful than he thought possible, "which would give us another hundred kilos leeway."

"More than that," said the literal-minded Nev and then gawped at the lieutenant. "Oh, you mean just the women's stuff."

"No," Ni Morgana said on a gusty sigh. "They've suffered enough from Kimmer. I don't see the point in further retribution."

"If it hadn't been for the extra fuel, we wouldn't have lifted off the planet," Nev suddenly remarked.

"If it hadn't been for the extra fuel, I don't think we'd've had this trouble with Kimmer," Ni Morgana said sardonically.

"He'd've tried something else," Benden said. "He'd planned the contingency of rescue a long, long time. Those vests and pants weren't whipped up overnight. Not with everything else those women were doing."

"That's possible," Ni Morgan said thoughtfully. "He was a crafty old bugger. All along he counted on our rescuing him. And he'd know we'd have to check body weight."

"D'you suppose he also fooled us," Nev asked anxiously, "about there being more survivors somewhere?"

That thought had been like a pain in Benden's guts since Kimmer's duplicity

had come to light. And yet — there *had* been no sign of other survivors on the southern continent. Nor had their instruments given them any positive readings as they spiraled across the snowy northern landmass. Then there was Shensu's story and that man had no reason to lie. Benden shook his head wearily and once again regarded the ship's digital. The search had taken a lot longer than he'd realized.

"Look alive," he said, rising to his feet with as good an appearance of energy as he could muster. "Nev, try to raise the *Amherst* again." He knew beforehand that the *Amherst* was unlikely to be receiving. He also knew that he had to alter the course *now*, before they went too far along the aborted trajectory. He didn't have any option. He made his calculations for the appropriate roll to get the *Erica* on the new flight path. He'd worry about contacting the *Amherst* later. He couldn't wait on this correction any longer. A three second burn at 1-g would do it. That wouldn't take up much fuel. And he breathed a silent prayer of thanksgiving. "Nev, Greene, Vartry, check our passengers. We've got to burn to our new heading in two minutes forty-five seconds."

He felt better after the burn. The gig was handling easily again. Like the thoroughbred she was, she had eased onto her new heading. And he had done something positive about their perilous situation.

"Now, let's be sure we get every last strip Kimmer added to the *Erica*," he said, unbuckling his seat restraints. He'd also go through the gig with an eye to what else could be jettisoned. But they'd a long trip ahead of them and precious few comforts for those on board.

"I'll check the women first," Ni Morgana said, pushing herself off deftly from the back of her couch and grabbing the hand hold to propel herself down the companionway. "And see about some grub. Breakfast was a long time ago."

Benden realized how right she was but, under stress, he never noticed hunger pangs. He did now. "Chow's the best idea yet," he said and managed a reasonably cheerful grin for her.

When she checked the women, she found them still shaken by the emotional prelude and, though they helped her in the galley, they were apathetic. Chio wept silently, ignoring the food Faith tried to get her to eat. She seemed wrapped in so deep a depression that Saraidh reported her condition to Benden.

"She won't last the journey in this condition, Ross," Saraidh said. "She's deeply disturbed and I don't think it's losing Kimmer."

"Isn't it just that she was so dependent on him? You heard what Shensu said."

"Well, if it is, we ought to sort it out. We can't avoid discussing Kimmer's demise."

"I know and I don't intend to. His demise," and he drawled out the euphemism, "was accidental. I would have preferred to have him alive and standing trial for his attempt to disable the *Erica*,"

168

Benden replied grimly.

"What I want to know is how he got those women to sabotage us. They must have known from our conversations that their extra mass would seriously burden the ship!"

Shensu had floated down the corridor during the last sentence and he gave them a terse nod.

"You must explain to my sisters that the gemstones alone will provide suitably for them," he said, "that the stones will not be confiscated by the Fleet to pay for this rescue."

"What?" Ni Morgana exclaimed. "Where did they get that notion?" She held up her hand. "Never mind. I know. Kimmer. What maggots had he got in his brain?"

"The maggot of greed," Shensu said. "Come, reassure my sisters. They are so fearful. They only cooperated with him on the metal because he said that would be the only wealth left to them."

"And how did Kimmer plan to remove all that platinum from the *Erica*?"

Benden demanded, knowing that his voice was rising in frustration but unable to stifle it. "The man was deranged."

"Quite likely," Shensu said with a shrug. "For decades he has clung to the hope that his message would be answered. Or else all he had accumulated, the gems, the metals, meant nothing."

They had reached the marines' quarters and heard Chio's soft weeping.

"Get the kids out of here, Nev," Benden told the ensign in a low voice, "and amuse them. Shensu, ask your sisters to join us here and, by whatever you hold sacred, tell them we mean them no harm."

IT TOOK HOURS TO REASSURE THE four women. Benden stuck to his matter of fact, common sense approach.

"Please believe me," he said with genuine concern at Chio's almost total collapse, "that the Fleet has special regulations about castaways or stranded persons. Stranded you were. It would be totally different if the Colonial Authority or Federated Headquarters had organized an official search, then there would have been staggering retrieval costs. But the *Amherst* only happened to be in the area and the system was orange-flagged . . ."

"And because," Ni Morgana took up the explanation, "I was doing research on the Oort cloud, Captain Fargoe ordered the gig to investigate. As she will tell you herself when you meet her, it saves you, the surviving colonists, any cost."

Chio mumbled something.

"Say again?" Ni Morgana asked very gently, smiling reassurance.

"Kimmer said we would be paupers."

"With black diamonds? The rarest kind of all?" Ni Morgana managed to convey a depth of astonishment that surprised Benden. "And you've kilos of them among you. And those medicines, Faith," and the science officer turned to the one sister who appeared to be really listening to what was said, "especially that numbweed salve of yours. Why the

171

patents on that alone will buy you a penthouse in any Federation city. If that's where you want to live."

"The salve?" Sheer surprise animated Faith. "But it's common — "

"On Pern, perhaps, but I've a degree in alien pharmacopia and I've never come across anything as mild and effective as that," Ni Morgana assured her. "You did bring seed as well as salve because I don't think that's the sort of medication that can be artificially reproduced and provide the same effect."

"We had to gather the leaves and boil them for hours," Hope said wonderingly. "The stink made it a miserable job but he made us do it each year."

"And numbweed can make us rich?" Charity doubted what she heard.

"I have no reason to lie to you," Ni Morgana said with such dignity that the girl flushed.

"But Kimmer is dead," Chio said, a sob catching in her throat and she turned her head away, her shoulders shaking.

"He is dead of greed," Kimo said in

an implacable voice. "And we are alive, Chio. We can make new lives for ourselves and do what we want to do now."

"That would be very nice," Faith said in a low wistful voice.

"We won't be Kimmer's slaves anymore," Kimo added.

"We would all have died without Kimmer after Mother died," Chio turned back, mastering her tears, unable to stop defending the man who had dominated her for so long.

"Died because she had too many stillborn babies," Kimo said. "You forget that, Chio. You forget that you were pregnant two months after you became a woman. You forget how you cried. I do not."

Chio stared at her brother, her face a mask of sorrow. Then she turned to Benden and Ni Morgana, her eyes narrow. "And will you tell this captain of yours about Kimmer's death?"

"Yes, we will naturally have to mention that unfortunate incident in our report," Benden said.

"And who killed him?" she shot the question at them both.

"We don't know who killed him, or if he cycled the lock open himself."

Chio was startled as if that possibility had not occurred to her until then. She pulled at Kimo's sleeve. "Is that possible?"

Kimo shrugged. "He believed his own lies, Chio. Once the metal was found, he would consider himself to be poor. He was at least honorable enough to commit suicide."

"Yes, honorable," Chio murmured so softly her words were barely audible. "I am tired. I wish to sleep." She turned herself toward the wall.

Kimo gave the two officers a nod of triumph. Faith covered her elder sister and gestured for them to leave.

OVER THE NEXT SEVERAL DAYS, passengers and crew settled into an easier relationship. The youngsters would sit for hours in front of the tri-d screen, going through the gig's library of tapes.

174

Saraidh cajoled Chio and the girls into watching some of them as well, as a gentle introduction to the marvels of modern high-tech civilization.

"I can't tell whether they're reassured or scared witless," she reported to Benden, standing his watch at the gig's console. They still had not made contact with the *Amherst* though he had no real cause for worry on that score — yet. "How many times have you worked those equations, Ross?" she asked, noticing what he had on his pad.

"Often enough to know there's no mathematical error," he said with a wry grin. "We'll only have the one chance."

"I'm not worried," she said with a shrug and a smile. "Off you get. It's my watch." And she shooed him out of the cabin.

"LIEUTENANT?" NEV'S VOICE REverberated excitedly down the companionway the next afternoon, "I've raised the *Amherst*!"

There was a cheer as Ross propelled

himself to the cabin.

"Neither loud nor clear, sir, but definitely voice contact," Nev said with a grin as if he himself were responsible for the deed.

Ross grinned back at him in relief and depressed the talk toggle on his seat arm. "Ross Benden reporting, sir. We need to make a new rendezvous."

Fargoe's voice acknowledged him and, though her tone broke up in transmission, he really didn't need to hear every syllable to know what she said.

"Ma'am, we've had to abort our original course. We are currently aiming for a slingshot around the first planet."

"You want a sunburn, Benden?"

"No, ma'am, but we have only 2.3 kps of Delta V remaining."

"How did you cut it that fine?"

"Humanitarian reasons required us to rescue the ten remaining survivors of the expedition."

"Ten?" There was a pause that had nothing to do with interference on the line. "I shall be very interested in your report, Benden. That is, if your humanitarianism allows you to make it. What is the total of the excess weight you're carrying?"

Nev handed over his pad and Benden read off the figures.

"Hmm. Off-hand I don't think we can match orbits. Can you make it five kps?"

"No, ma'am."

"Roger. Hold on while we refigure your course and rendezvous point."

Benden tried not to look toward Nev or at Saraidh who had joined them at the command console. He tried not to look nervous but felt various parts of himself twitching, unusual enough in gravity and damned annoying in free-fall. He clutched the edge of the console as unobtrusively and as hard as possible to keep from twitching out of the chair.

"*Erica*? Captain Fargoe here. What can you jettison?"

"How much is required?" Benden thought of the wealth they had just consigned to space.

177

"You've got to jettison 49.05 kilos. You will need to make a 10-g burn for 1.3 seconds around the first planet, commencing at 91 degrees right ascension. That will put you on course, speed and direction and, we devoutly hope, in time to make a new rendezvous. Good luck, Lieutenant." Her voice indicated that he'd need it.

He didn't like 10-g, even for 1.3 seconds. They'd all black out. It'd be rough on the kids. But it'd be a lot rougher to turn into cinders.

"You heard the captain," he said, turning first to Saraidh and then Nev. "Let's snap to it."

"What'll we toss, Lieutenant?" Nev asked.

"Just about everything that isn't bolted down," Saraidh said, "and probably some of that. I'll start in the galley."

In the end they made up the required kilos out of material which Saraidh knew could be most easily replaced by stores from the *Amherst*: extra power packs, oxygen tanks which accounted for a good deal of the necessary weight, the mess-room table, and all but one of the beacon missiles which the gig carried.

"If Captain Fargoe decides you weren't negligent," Saraidh told Ross, her face expressionless, as they both watched the articles sliding out of the airlock into space, "you won't have to pay for 'em."

"What?" Then he saw she was teasing and grinned back at her. "I've enough I've got to account for, thank you muchly, ma'am, on this expedition without paying for it, too." He kept trying to explain Kimmer's demise to himself and how he could have prevented it, if he could have.

"Now, now, Ross," and Saraidh waggled a finger at him. They were alone in the corridor. "Don't hang Kimmer about your neck. I subscribe completely with the suicide theory. Temporarily of unsound mind due to the failure of his plan. He might just have done it to be awkward, too."

"I'm not sure Captain Fargoe would

buy that one."

"Ah, but she'd never met Kimmer, and I have," and Saraidh gave him an encouraging thumbs-up.

THE MOMENT OF TRUTH CAME two long weary weeks later. The temperature inside the *Erica* began to rise with their proximity to Rukbat's sun, reaching an uncomfortable level. Benden was sweating heavily as he watched the ominous approach of the tiny black cinder of the system's first planet. That poor wight hadn't had a chance to survive. He intended to.

"Burn minus sixty seconds," he announced over the intercom. He hadn't informed his passengers of the rigors of a slingshot maneuver. They'd all black out and, if something went wrong, they'd never know it. Meanwhile, he hadn't had to endure Chio's suspicions or the sorrowful reproaches of the other three women. He'd done slingshot passages before, both actual and in simulation. It was more a matter of timing the burn properly just as the ninety-one degree right ascension came up on the nav screen. He just hated blacking out for any reason, not being in control for those seconds or minutes.

"Nine, eight, seven," chanted Nev, his eyes glittering with anticipation. This was his first slingshot. "Five, four, three, two . . . one!"

Benden pressed the burn button, and the *Erica* lunged forward willingly. As he was slammed deep into the pads of the contour seat, he knew the maneuver would be successful and surrendered to the mighty g-forces he had just initiated.

BENDEN RETURNED TO CONsciousness, the blessed silence of space and the relief of weightlessness. His first glance was for the expended fuel. Point ninety-eight kps left. It should be enough. Provided the course corrections were accurate. He had one last burn to make as they bisected the *Amherst*'s wake and then turned back to her at a sharp vector.

"My compliments, Lieutenant," Ni Morgana said briskly, unsnapping her harness. "We seem to be well on our way now. I think the cook has something special for lunch today."

Benden blinked at her.

She grinned. "The very same thing we had yesterday for lunch."

Benden wasn't the only one who groaned. They'd added supplies at Honshu, but the fresh foods were long gone and they were down to the emergency rations: nourishing but uninspired. And that's all they had for the next two weeks. When he was back on board the *Amherst*, Ross Benden was going to order up the most lavish celebratory meal in the mess's well-stocked larder. 'When,' and he grinned to himself. That's positive thinking.

When the *Erica*'s sensors picked up the cruiser's unmistakable ion radiation trail, Benden was in the command cabin, teaching Alun and Pat the elements of spatial navigation. The boys were bright and so eager to prepare themselves for their new life that they were a pleasure to instruct.

"Back to your pads, boys. We've got another burn."

"Like the last one?" Alun asked plaintively.

"No, matey. Not like the last one. Just a touch on the button."

Reassured, they propelled themselves out of the cabin and down the companionway, dexterously passing Saraidh and Nev at the door.

"A touch being all the fuel we've got left," Saraidh murmured, taking her seat. She leaned forward, peering out into the blackness of space around them.

"You won't see anything yet," Nev remarked.

"I know it," she replied, shrugging. "Just looking."

"It's there, though."

"And not long gone," Benden added, "judging by the strength of the ion count." He toggled on the intercom. "Now listen up. A short burn, not like the last, just enough to change our

183

course to match up our final approach to the *Amherst*." In an aside to Saraidh he added, "I feel like a damned leisure liner captain."

"You'd make a grand one," she replied blandly, "especially if you have to change your branch of service."

"My what?" Benden never knew when Lieutenant Ni Morgana's wayward humor would erupt.

"Lighten up, Ross. We're nearly home and dry."

"Fifteen minutes to course correction." He nodded to Nev to watch the digital while he contacted the *Amherst*. "*Erica* to *Amherst*. Do you read me?"

"Loud and clear," came Captain Fargoe's voice. "About ready to join us, Lieutenant?"

"That's my aim, Captain."

"We'll trust it's as accurate as ever. Fire when ready, Gridley."

"Captain?"

"Roger, over and out."

Beside him, Saraidh was chuckling. "Where does she get them?"

"Get what?" asked Nev.

"Are you counting down, Ensign?"

"Yes, sir. Coming down to ten minutes forty seconds."

Why was it time could be so elastic? Benden wondered as the ten minutes seemed to go on forever, clicking second by second. At the minute, he flexed both hands, shook his shoulders to release the tension in his neck. At zero, he depressed the burn on the last ninety-eight kps in the tank, yawing to starboard. He felt the surge of the good gig *Erica* as she responded. Then all of a sudden the engines cut out with the exhausted whoosh that meant no more fuel in the tank.

Had the *Erica* completed the course correction? Or had the engines stopped untimely? The margin was so damned slight! And the proof would be the appearance of the comforting bulk of the *Amherst* any time now. If the maneuver had been completed before the fuel was exhausted.

Like the two officers beside him,

185

Benden instinctively leaned forward, peering out into the endless space in front of them.

"I've got a radar reading, Lieutenant," Nev said and there was no denying the relief in his voice. "It can't be anything but the *Amherst*. I think we're going to make it."

"All we need is to get close enough for them to shoot us a magnetic line," Benden muttered.

Nev uttered a whoop. "Thar she be!" and he pointed. Benden had to blink to be sure he actually was seeing the running lights of the *Amherst*. He was close to adding his own kiyi of relief and victory.

Just then the com-unit opened to a sardonic voice. "That's cutting it fine indeed, Lieutenant." The blank screen cleared to a view of the captain, her head cocked and her right eyebrow quizzically aslant. "Trying to match your uncle's finesse?"

"Not consciously, ma'am, I assure you, but I'd be pleased to hear the confirmation that our present course and speed are a-ok for docking?"

"Not a puff of fuel left, huh?"

"No, ma'am."

She looked to her left, then faced the screen squarely again, a little smile playing on her lips. "You'll make it. And I'll expect to have reports from both you and Lieutenant Ni Morgana as soon as you've docked. You've had time enough on the trip in to write a hundred reports."

"Captain, I've got the passengers to settle."

"They'll be settled by medics, Ross. You've done your part getting them here. I want to see those reports."

And the screen darkened.

"Got yours all ready, Ross?" Ni Morgana asked with a sly grin as she swiveled her chair around.

"Yes. What about yours?"

"Oh, it's ready, too. I said that I believed Kimmer suicided."

Benden nodded, glad of her support. "It would have had to have been self-destruction, Saraidh. He would have been far more familiar with airlock controls than Shensu or his brothers," Benden said slowly, considering his words. "It's really far more likely that he did suicide, given the fact that he had failed to bring along all that metal. Damn fool! He must have known that he was dangerously overloading the ship. He could have murdered us." That angered Benden.

"Yes, and nearly succeeded. I think he was hoping that his death would have brought suspicion on the brothers as the most likely to wish his demise," Ni Morgana went on. "He would have liked jeopardizing their futures. And discrediting another Benden if he could." When she heard Benden's sharp inhalation, she touched his hand, causing him to look at her. "You can still be proud of your uncle, Ross. You heard what Shensu said, and how proud he was of the way the admiral marshaled all available defenses."

Benden cocked his head, his expression rueful. "A fighter to the last . . . and

188

it took a wretched planet to defeat him."

"Poor planet Pern," Saraidh said sadly. "Not its fault but I'm recommending that this system be interdicted. I did some calculations — which I'll verify on the *Amherst* computers — and rechecked the original EEC report. That wasn't the first time the Oort organism fell on the planet. Nor will it be the last. It'll happen every 250 years, give or take a decade. Furthermore, we don't want any ship blundering into that Oort cloud and transporting that organism to other systems."

She gave a shudder at the thought.

"There she is," Benden said with a sense of relief as the viewport filled with the perceptibly nearing haven of the Amherst. "And, all things considered, a successful rescue run."

THE END